Good Morning, Miss Dove

Goo[d]

ILLUSTRATED BY

GARRETT PRICE

Morning, Miss Dove

by FRANCES GRAY PATTON
AUTHOR OF THE FINER THINGS OF LIFE

Dodd, Mead & Company · New York

TO MARY HENDREN VANCE

Liberty Hill was a small freshwater town—not a hill, really, but just a modest rise in the land—where the streets were named for trees and heroes, and a sense of life's continuity ran in the air. It was like a hundred American towns, smug and cozy, and it put its special stamp upon its own. People born and raised there— high and low, rich and poor—were neighbors in an irrevocable way, because their imaginations had been nursed on the same sights and sounds and legends and early ordeals. They had played in the same sunny fields and cooled off after the heat of their games in the same shade. They had grown up hearing the same courthouse clock tell the hours and the quarters in a tone as timeless as time itself. They had all, for the space of a whole generation, been exposed at a tender and malleable age to the impartial justice, the ada-mantine regulations, and the gray, calm, neutral eyes of the same teacher—the terrible Miss Dove.

This community of experience was absorbed, of course, into the stream of consciousness. It was so settled, so accustomed, that it seemed a manifestation of natural law. Like the dew on the grass or the return of morning light (that recurrent miracle that passes for a commonplace) it excited no wonder. But if the light had failed to return, if the voice of the clock had fallen silent—even in the night when its sound was muffled by dreams—then people would have heard the silence and noticed the darkness. So when, without warning, the tenor of Miss Dove's existence was interrupted, and she was seen, at an hour when she should have graced the geography room at Cedar Grove School, being borne down the sidewalks in the direction of the hospital—then Liberty Hill caught its breath, and looked beneath the surface of its life and fastened its hand upon its heart.

The Wednesday upon which Miss Dove took sick began in an ordinary way. It was mid-April. The weather was mild. The sun rose at five-twenty-five, two minutes earlier than it had risen on Tuesday—which was precisely what Miss Dove had predicted the afternoon before when, shining a flashlight on a plaster-of-paris globe, she had demonstrated to the sixth grade the reason for the lengthening of the vernal days. During the night a flock of robins had returned from their southern winter resort (Miss Dove had told the first grade this was the week for the robins) and now they were busy pulling innocent angle-worms from new-spaded garden plots, looking spruce and pompous and complacent—as if they knew they were

2

expected and thought the worm-rich earth had been loosened expressly for their benefit. At seven, households stirred. Families, groggy from dreams, fought among themselves for the bathroom. Lost socks were hunted, ears were scrubbed, hair was combed, milk was spilt and the air was rent with squeals and remonstrances and the resumption of those domestic hostilities which, in general, keep personal identity alive. At seven minutes past eight—punctual as the sun and, unlike the sun, not varying with the seasons—Miss Dove descended the front steps of her house on Oakwood Street. At her gate she paused for a moment. She looked at three fat robins in her pansy border—not severely but strictly, as she might have looked at children to see how they were occupied; she observed, with a slight frown, a dandelion blooming out of place on her lawn; she lifted a critical gaze to the sky and, seeing that it was quite clean, gave a nod of approval. Then she opened her gate—it was an old gate made of wrought-iron in a Victorian pattern of hearts and ferns but it did not squeak because Miss Dove kept its hinges oiled—and began her morning walk to Cedar

Grove Elementary School.

Jincey Baker saw her from an upstairs window. Jincey was eating breakfast in bed, not because she was ill or lazy but because she was going to have a baby any time now and she was young and beautiful and her husband liked to pamper her.

"There she goes, Tommy!" Jincey cried on that note of delight with which she often singularized the trivial or accustomed. "Right on the dot!" She patted her stomach. "I wish little Whosit—the slow-poke— would copy Miss Dove and develop a sense of time!"

Tommy (Dr. Thomas Baker, surgeon) laughed. "It would be a strain, though, to have a baby like the terrible Miss Dove. Imagine burping it!"

"Do you suppose *she* ever was a baby?" Jincey said.

"No," Thomas replied flatly. "She simply emerged from her house one day—fully formed like Venus on the half-shell."

"With her hat on?" said Jincey.

"Of course," said Thomas.

"And her mousey hair in a little bun behind?"

"I'm not sure," said Thomas. "You see, I have a unique distinction. I'm the only man in Liberty Hill who's ever seen the terrible Miss Dove with her hair down."

"Tommy!" Jincey clapped her hands. "You kept it from me!"

"Oh, I have my reticence," Thomas said darkly. "And that is a solemn memory."

"Tell me now," demanded Jincey.

"I'll save it for a long winter evening when we can't get a baby sitter," Thomas said. "I have to tear myself away now 'from your chaste nunnery'. She has already passed which means I'm late for rounds. I'll be home for lunch unless some rash fool bursts an appendix."

"Stop at the Burnhams' and pick up the bathinet they're lending us," said Jincey.

"Sure. And if anything happens—if you have the slightest twinge—don't dally. The hospital's alerted for you." He bent and pressed his cheek against her soft, sweet-smelling red hair. "Don't worry, darling."

"I'm not worried," Jincey said. "Are you?"

"Of course not," Thomas said with more than necessary emphasis. He straightened up, squared his shoulders, and assumed a professional nonchalance. "It's a normal physiological process."

He ran downstairs whistling an optimistic tune from *Oklahoma* and thinking with remorse of all the prospective fathers he had privately jeered at. Those wan creatures with their stubble cheeks and dying-calf eyes, pacing the halls, needing a drink—they were his brothers now! "If she's all right—if the child's recognizably human—" he promised Something, "—I vow I'll—" But what bargain could he make? He was a young man of exemplary habits. He had no major vice—not even a grandiose sense of sin—to sacrifice in propitiation of the gods.

At nine minutes past eight Miss Dove crossed La-Fayette Avenue. Old Mr. Porter, who had been her father's friend, saw her from his flag-stone terrace where he was taking his preprandial constitutional. He checked his watch by her. At eighty-two, Mr. Porter was an epicure of time. He relished it, unseasoned, for its own essential flavor.

A few minutes later, from the window of a dining room facing on Maple Street, Polly Burnham saw Miss Dove go by. "Finish your oatmeal, Davie-dear," she said to her nine-year-old son. "Miss Dove has

6

passed. You don't want to be tardy."

"Oh, puke," said Davie-dear. "The oatmeal stinks!"

Polly flushed but held her peace. Her husband, the Reverend Alexander Burnham, was aware of a curious tingling sensation in the palm of his right hand and a nearly irrepressible longing to bring that palm down, wham, in a series of blows upon a plump portion of his son's anatomy. He rose. "If you'll excuse me," he said to his wife, "I must go over my notes for the vestry meeting." He scuttled off to his study, marveling at his self-restraint.

Both the elder Burnhams knew that in gently-nurtured children, rough language was a healthy sign—a sign of growth and toughening of the ego. They knew, furthermore, that David, because he resembled one of Raphael's cherubs and was a minister's son, had more need than most for toughness. Parents must bow to the wind and pretend not to notice. All the books said that.

At eight-twenty, Miss Dove crossed to the corner of Maple and Grant, where Cedar Grove School sat— redbrick, stolid, with only one cedar left to soften its ugliness, for its grove had been chopped down long before in the interests of level playgrounds Bill Holloway, the traffic cop on duty, saw her. "She looked as natural as nature," he reported later in a tone of wonder. "I tipped my cap and said: 'Good morning, Miss Dove' and she says, genteel like always, 'Good morning, William.' "

By eight-thirty, some two hundred and fifty children, ranging in age from six to twelve, were safely inside the school building. In various home-rooms they gauged, with the uncanny shrewdness of innocence, the various moods of various teachers. How far dared they go today?

But as the morning progressed and the classes went, in turn, to spend forty-five minutes in the geography room with Miss Dove, they dropped their restless speculation.

For Miss Dove had no moods. Miss Dove was a certainty. She would be today what she had been yesterday and would be tomorrow. And so, within limits, would they. Single file they would enter her room. Each child would pause on the threshold as its mother and father had paused, more than likely, and would say—just as the policeman had said—in distinct, formal accents: "Good morning, Miss Dove." And Miss Dove would look directly at each of them, fixing her eyes directly upon theirs, and reply: "Good morning, Jessamine," or "Margaret," or "Samuel." (Never "Sam," never "Peggy," never "Jess." She eschewed familiarity as she wished others to eschew it.) They would go to their appointed desks. Miss Dove would

8

ascend to hers. The lesson would begin.

There was no need to waste time in preliminary admonitions. Miss Dove's rules were as fixed as the signs of the zodiac. And they were known. Miss Dove rehearsed them at the beginning of each school year, stating them as calmly and dispassionately as if she were describing the atmospheric effects of the Gulf Stream. The penalties for infractions of the rules were also known. If a child introduced a foreign object—a pencil, let us say, or a wad of paper, or a lock of hair—into his mouth, he was required to wash out his mouth with the yellow laundry soap that lay on the drain-

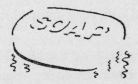

board of the sink in the corner by the sand table. If his posture was incorrect he had to go and sit for a while upon a stool without a back-rest. If a page in his notebook was untidy, he had to copy it over. If he emitted an uncovered cough, he was expected to rise immediately and fling open a window, no matter how cold the weather, so that a blast of fresh air could protect his fellows from the contamination of his germs. And if he felt obliged to disturb the class routine by leaving the room for a drink of water (Miss Dove loftily ignored any other necessity) he did so to an accompaniment of dead silence. Miss Dove would

9

look at him—that was all—following his departure and greeting his return with her perfectly expressionless gaze and the whole class would sit idle and motionless, until he was back in the fold again. It was easier—even if one had eaten salt fish for breakfast—to remain and suffer.

Of course, there were flagrant offenses that were dealt with in private. Sometimes profanity sullied the air of the geography room. Sometimes, though rarely, open rebellion was displayed. In those instances, the delinquent was detained, minus the comfort of his comrades, in awful seclusion with Miss Dove. What happened between them was never fully known. (Did she threaten him with legal prosecution? Did she beat him with her long map-pointer?) The culprit, himself, was unlikely to be communicative on the subject or, if he were, to overdo the business with a tale that revolved to an incredible degree around his own heroism. Afterward, as was duly noted, his classroom attitude was subdued and chastened.

Miss Dove had no rule relating to prevarication. A child's word was taken at face value. If it happened to be false—well, that was the child's problem. A lie, unattacked and undistorted by defense, remained a lie and was apt to be recognized as such by its author.

Occasionally a group of progressive mothers would contemplate organized revolt. "She's been teaching too long," they would cry. "Her pedagogy hasn't changed since we were in Cedar Grove. She rules the children through fear!" They would turn to the boldest one among themselves. "*You* go," they would say. "You go talk to her!"

The bold one would go, but somehow she never did much talking. For there in the geography room, she would begin to feel—though she wore her handsomest tweeds and perhaps a gardenia for courage—that she was about ten years old and her petticoat was showing. Her throat would tickle. She would wonder desperately if she had a clean handkerchief in her bag. She would also feel thirsty. Without firing a shot in the cause of freedom she would retreat ingloriously from the field of battle.

And on that unassaulted field—in that room where no leeway was given to the personality, where a thing was black or white, right or wrong, polite or rude, simply because Miss Dove said it was, there was a curiously soothing quality. The children left it refreshed and restored, ready for fray or frolic. For within its walls they enjoyed what was allowed them nowhere else—a complete suspension of will.

On this particular Wednesday the first-graders, to whom Miss Dove gave a survey course in the flora and fauna of the Earth, drew pictures of robins. They drew them in crayon on eight-by-eleven sheets of manila paper. They did not draw them from memory. They copied the bird Miss Dove had drawn for them on the blackboard. (She knew exactly how a robin looked and saw no sense in permitting her pupils to rely upon their own random observations.) They left an inch-wide margin, measuring it with a ruler, around each picture. (Miss Dove believed in margins—except for error!) All the first-grade's robins would look alike.

Which was as it should be. Which was true of robins everywhere. Miss Dove was concerned with facts, not with artistic impressions.

She divided the second-grade into activity groups. One group cut scenic photographs from old magazines and pasted them in a scrapbook. Another modeled clay caribou for the sand table. Still another drew a colored mural on the rear blackboard. The groups did not talk among themselves, asking questions and pooling advice. They had no need to. Miss Dove had told them what to do.

The third grade recited the states of the Union. It was Miss Dove's experience that the eight-year-old mind learned best by rote.

At a quarter past eleven the fourth grade filed in. This grade was studying economic geography—the natural resources of different regions and their manifold uses in civilized life—and on Monday was to take a proficiency test prepared by the state Board of Education. Each year in April all grammar-grade students —students in the fourth, fifth and sixth grades—were so examined. Regarding these tests, Miss Dove's sentiments were mixed. She resented them as an intrusion upon her privacy and as an implication that her efficiency was open to question. But she recognized in them, grudgingly, a certain practice-value to the children.

For in every life—once, if not oftener—there was a proficiency test. A time came when one was put to the proof. One stood alone. He was what he was. He knew what he knew. He did what he could. And he had no source of strength outside himself. Certainly, such a time had come to Miss Dove.

And on a plane more human than sublime, Miss Dove's vanity had always been flattered by the results of the test. Cedar Grove led the state in geography.

"You may utilize this period for review, children," she said. "Open your books to page ninety-three. Memorize the agricultural products of the Argentine pampas."

At that moment Miss Dove was first aware of a pain in her back. The pain was small in area but it was acute. It thrust like a knife into her spine. It was so intense, so unfamiliar, and so unexpected that she hardly believed in it. It descended along her right thigh. Miss Dove counted ten. The pain was easier. It was gone. It had been only a threat.

Tension, she thought. Anxiety about the proficiency tests. She was displeased with herself. She despised women who had backaches. *I must tranquilize my mind,* she told herself. *I will think of the Alps. White. Clean. Lofty. Rising above Lake Lucerne. The lake is blue; it reflects the evening star.* So she concentrated her thoughts upon mountains and water that she had never seen. And after a while she was sure she had imagined that stab of agony in her spine.

She slipped a rubber band from a sheaf of fifth grade essay papers. She took a red pencil and began to correct them. But part of her mind stayed with the class that was present. She knew, for instance, when Vicky Evans, who was disposed to day-dreams, tired of her book and started gazing out the window. "Come back, Victoria," she said.

She heard when David Burnham sighed and muttered something exceedingly improper under his breath. "Hell and damn," David said.

"You will remain after class, David," Miss Dove said without glancing up from the fifth grade papers.

"Yes, Miss Dove," said David.

At noon an electric buzzer, operated from a switch in the principal's office, shrilled through Cedar Grove School. It was the signal for lunch and "big recess." In almost every room children slammed their books shut, shuffled their feet, sloshed their paint-water, and made a mass lunge toward food and freedom. Different teachers reacted according to their different temperaments. The art teacher, for instance, was a full-blown, husky girl who had been a college hockey star as well as an esthetics major. She made a flying leap

15

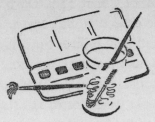

and reached the door ahead of her class. "Clean your paint brushes!" she yelled. "Police up your desks!" Her thick, wiry hair stood out around her face and—so the enchanted children claimed—was heard to crackle. "It's nothing to me if you starve!" The music teacher began to play the piano. "Softly, softly!" she begged in her sweet, tinkly voice. "Trippingly on our toes! Let's all be elves and fairies!" The literature teacher was not sorry to be interrupted; she had been reading aloud from *Hiawatha*, a work she considered unworthy of her critical talents. She shrugged, not caring what the children did so long as they went away, and began a letter to her fiance who was pursuing his doctorate at Purdue. "Lover," she wrote, "I am sinking in an intellectual quagmire."

But in the geography room there was no disorder. Forty-three children sat quietly in their places. They did not look up. Their posture was superb. Their brows were puckered in thought as they read on of wheat and beef and leather. From this room they were not to be becked or called by mechanical noises. Here they acknowledged one sole authority which, in due time, would speak.

"Attention, please," said Miss Dove in the serene voice of one who expects to be obeyed.

Forty-three children folded their hands on their desks and raised limpid eyes to her face.

"Close your books, please," said Miss Dove.

Forty-three books were closed, not slammed, in the respectful manner due to books.

"The class will rise," said Miss Dove.

The class rose. So did its teacher. The pain returned. It nibbled at a vertebra like some small rodent with sharp, burrowing teeth. But it was bearable, as most things are in moments sustained by duty.

Miss Dove continued standing there on her raised platform as she did at the end of every class period. (To sit down would be to show weakness. And no teacher, Miss Dove was convinced, could afford to show weakness if she wished her pupils to show strength.) On the desk before her, like an orb and scepter, were her map-pointer and her globe. On the wall behind her, like a tapestry depicting far-flung dominions, hung the map of the world.

"The class is dismissed," said Miss Dove.

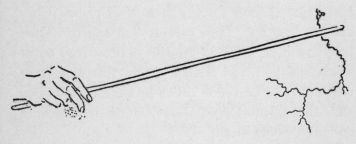

Forty-two children, one by one—without scrambling or pushing—filed out into the hall. David Burnham remained standing in the aisle.

For an instant Miss Dove was tempted to let David go with the others—to excuse him with a reprimand or, at least, to defer his punishment until the next day. If she could rest during the whole lunch hour, sitting perfectly still and even (though the notion was unorthodox) putting her head down upon her desk— But no. David's character was in her keeping.

Miss Dove understood, quite as well as David's parents did, the child's motivation. (She had taught other ministers' sons.) But unlike them she did not care whether David loved or hated her. She cared only that he conform to the rules.

She had pondered the new psychology which held that in the depths of human nature lay wild-animal instincts of greed, anger, idleness, and discourtesy. She could credit that theory. She had no rosy concept of human nature. But what did the theory prove? The thing that distinguished a man from a brute—a gentleman from a savage—was not instinct but performance.

David knew she had heard his naughty oath. He had meant her to hear it. In vulgar parlance, he had "asked for it" and he had a right to "get it."

Miss Dove looked at David. Her gaze was not contemptuous. Not impressed. She saw no hero in the aisle and no monster, either. She saw a nine-year-old boy who had gone a little further than he now wished he had.

And what did David see as he looked at Miss Dove? How did any of Miss Dove's pupils, past or present, see her? Off hand, that would seem an easy question. There was nothing elusive about Miss Dove's appearance and it had, moreover, remained much the same for more than thirty-five years. When she had begun to teach geography her figure had been spare and angular

and it was still so. Her hair was more shadowy than it had once been but, twisted into a meagre little old-maid's-knot, it had never had a chance to show much color. Her thin, unpainted mouth bore no sign of those universal emotions—humor, for instance, and love, and uncertainty—that mark most mouths in the course of time. Her pale, bleached-out complexion never flushed with emotion—a slight pinkness at the tip of her pointed nose was the only visible indication that ordinary human blood ran through her veins.

She wore round-toed black shoes with low, rubber-tapped heels that did not clatter when she walked. Her dress, of some dull-surfaced dark material, was close cousin to the one in which she had made her pedagogical debut: It had the same long sleeves, the same high neck, and the same white linen handkerchief (or one very like) fluted into a fan and pinned to its left bosom. (The handkerchief was not for use —Miss Dove did not cough or sneeze in public—, nor was it for ornament. It was a caution to its owner's pupils that it behooved each of them to possess a clean handkerchief, too.) All in all, in bearing and clothing and bony structure, Miss Dove suggested that classic portrait of the eternal teacher that small fry, generation after generation, draw upon fences and sidewalks with nubbins of purloined chalk; a grown-up stranger, catching his first glimpse of her, might be inclined to laugh with a kind of relief, as if he'd seen some old, haunting ogress of his childhood turned into a harmless joke. And then Miss Dove would look at him and all the comedy would ebb from his mind. Her large eyes were quite naked (for she had retained perfect vision) and gray like a flat, calm sea on a cloudy day. They were shrewd and unillusioned; and when one stood exposed to their scrutiny feeling uncomfortably that they penetrated veil upon veil of one's private life and perceived, without astonishment, many hidden—and often unlovely—truths in the deep recesses of one's nature, it was impossible to see anything about Miss Dove as ridiculous. Even the elevated position of her desk—a position deplored by modern educators who seek to introduce equality into the teacher-student relation—was right and proper. The dais of aloof authority suited her as a little hill near Ratisbon suited Napoleon Bonaparte.

But there was more to Miss Dove. There was something that defies analysis. She had an extra quality as compelling as personal charm (which she did *not* have and would have scorned to cultivate) that captured the imagination. She gave off a sort of effulgence of awe and terror. But the terror did not paralyze. It was terror that caused children to flex their moral muscles and to dream of enduring, without a whimper, prolonged ordeals of privation and fatigue. Sometimes, if their ideal of courage was high, it caused them even to dare Miss Dove's disapproval.

The little ones, the six-year olds, whose geographical primer was entitled "At Home with Birds and Beasts," often pictured Miss Dove in the guise of some magnificent creature, furred or feathered. She was a huge black grizzly reared on its hind legs to block a mountain pass; she was a camel—bigger than other camels—leading a caravan across the desert; she was a Golden Eagle on a crag in Scotland. Later, when they had progressed to the intellectual sophistication of the fourth, the fifth, or the sixth and final grade of Cedar Grove School they were likely to cast her in the image of symbol. (One fanciful child had likened her to the

21

Pharos watching little skiffs in the harbor of Alexandria.) But David Burnham was not fanciful; he was scared. Had he been pressed, at the moment, to describe Miss Dove, he would have said: "She looks like a teacher."

Miss Dove would have been gratified. A teacher was what she was and what she wished to be.

She had been under twenty when she had begun to teach—a reserved, hesitant girl whose deep romantic impulses had not yet caught fire. A girl who had felt calamity in one swift blow before she had felt more than a tentative "fluttering up toward joy." She had embraced her profession with the singleness of purpose that she might, under other circumstances, have bestowed upon matrimony, or foreign travel, or carving in stone.

Miss Dove's first youth had been a small-town American idyl. She was the eldest of three daughters in the first family of Liberty Hill. Her father, Alphonzo, was president of the bank—a witty, bookish man, more amiable than provident. Her mother was a fragile woman who smelled of violets and had the kind of gentle beauty that "trembles over children sleeping." Her two little sisters were like their mother. Miss Dove was like herself.

Though she was not so pretty as her mother and sisters, she was not entirely without a claim to vanity. Her figure was too spare for fashion, her expression too self-contained, but her carriage was superb and she had a cloud of soft, blowy hair, the color of sunshine sifting through pale brown leaves. She wore it gathered back, tied with a school-girl ribbon, long after she was old enough to pin it up. (Her father, whose special pet she was, had liked to see it hanging loose and in that innocent period of history a girl could cater to a parent's whim without the fear of being thought morbid.) She had, also, that innate appreciation of excellence which occurs, sui generis, in the morally elect.

The whole family admired her but it was her father who—having enjoyed the advantages of travel and being, in a dilettante way, a connoisseur of human nature—perceived most clearly the special quality of his daughter. It was a quality that should not be tampered with. It was like the delicate glaze that distinguishes fine porcelain from ordinary ware; like the bouquet of a vintage wine; like the star in the heart of a sapphire. Accordingly, he assumed responsibility for her early education. He taught her languages and the geography of the earth, ancient and modern. He introduced her to the genre of rare travel books which he collected at great expense. He read the poets with her—taking care to delete such passages as might offend her ear. He taught her to play chess and to dance and to ride (there was no girl in town who could sit a horse the way Miss Dove could), and he taught her to think well of herself. Above all, Mr. Dove delighted in expounding those sentiments of lofty principle and honor that he truly worshipped (though sometimes from afar!) and that his first-born child understood so well.

When she was eighteen she was sent off to school for a year of finishing. The school was a good one, built of gray stone turreted like a castle and set among spacious lawns overlooking a river. Once a week there was a party to which select young gentlemen were invited. At one of those functions, Miss Dove met a Princeton graduate student who was interested in archeology. He was taken with her and she, within ladylike bounds, with him. She allowed him to call upon her. They sat on a marble bench under a willow tree reading *The Last Days of Pompeii* and discoursing at intervals upon the glory of Greece and the grandeur of Rome.

In 1916, the summer she was nineteen, she "came out." She was presented to the simple, old-fashioned society of Liberty Hill in a simple, old-fashioned way. Her mother gave a tea to which the settled ladies of the town were invited. In a white dress—a charming dress of imported muslin and lace insertion—and with her hair still down, Miss Dove stood in the parlor and was introduced, in a new role, to her mother's friends.

She was no longer a child with a child's privileges and limitations. She was a young lady, a social entity in her own right. She was the grownup daughter of the house.

No, she was not pretty. She was still far too thin. Her nose was too pointed. Her eyes were too large for her face. But she had a look of elegance. Her bones were small. Her features were carven. Her complexion, though it wanted brilliance, had transparency. Her floating hair, like autumn water, caught the light. And she had another look—a young girl's "threshold look"—that could pierce the heart. She was poised, motionless for a moment in time, waiting for a sign from Life. Any time now, a poet might have said (if indeed, there had been a poet in that parlor), some inner leaven might begin to work in Miss Dove, the miraculous bloom and sheen of a girl's full springtime might flow through and over her and she might become anything at all. Whatever she did become was certain to be remarkable.

That evening her mother retired early. Miss Dove sat on in the parlor with her father. He had just received from his London book-dealer an exceedingly fine edition of Marco Polo's *Travels*. He took it to a table under a lamp. Miss Dove went to the piano. She began to play a Viennese waltz that her father liked. The room was full of roses and through the open window came the honey-rich scent of leaves and new-cut grass. Life seemed to stretch ahead in a suc-

cession of summer days. It would bear her smoothly, decorously, like the music of the waltz, to further and further realms of felicity. To balls, to horse-shows, to foreign cities. To—love?

In the bosom of her dress she had stuck a letter from the young archeologist. In it he asked leave to visit her in Liberty Hill. "Perhaps," he wrote, "our friendship begun under such happy auspices, will ripen into something warmer."

26

And then something—a deepening quiet in the room behind her or the sound of a barely audible sigh—made her whirl around on the piano stool. Her father was slumped forward. His cheek rested upon his open book, on a page describing the great wall of China. One arm lay flung out on the table, palm up, as if in a gesture of apology. Without a cry of farewell he had embarked upon the most mysterious journey that the soul of man can undertake.

Miss Dove did not take to her bed with a bromide as her dainty mother did, or weep, like her little sisters, in the arms of every matronly caller. Her grief was a walking paralysis. Yet she could have borne that grief. She could have borne, as well, her unexpected poverty (Mr. Dove had left his family only an annuity from a small trust fund), but there was a worse thing to bear. He had not left them a good name. Mr. Alphonzo Dove had lifted money from the bank.

Mr. Porter, her father's successor at the bank, told Miss Dove that on the evening after the funeral. He was obliged to tell someone in the family. He chose the eldest daughter whose numb composure he mistook for phlegm.

Miss Dove was sitting with him in the parlor when he told her. The room, she thought, was unchanged in a cruel, callous way. There were still roses in the vases and a beeswax luster on the furniture. But there was no music in the air and drawn blinds held the fragrance of the garden at bay. And Miss Dove's dress was black.

"Your father," said Mr. Porter, phrasing the matter delicately, "borrowed money without first observing the conventional forms."

Miss Dove's world began to whirl round and round, spinning itself into a dark, narrowing funnel.

"He *stole?*" she said.

Mr. Porter was shocked by the brutal word. Was the girl a monster? "Your father was my friend," he said.

"How much did he steal?" asked Miss Dove.

"He *borrowed* four or five thousand," Mr. Porter said. "In driblets here and there. No more than he could have hoped to return."

"Oh," said Miss Dove. To a pampered girl who had never had a defined allowance, the sum was astronomical.

"I want to manage this discreetly," Mr. Porter told her. "But I'm responsible to our depositors."

Miss Dove said nothing.

"Of course," he said, "the banking business is Caesar's wife." His glance, casual but appraising, went over the parlor. It touched the books behind the thirteen octagonal panes of the old highboy. "A valuable library," he said. It skimmed the wide floorboards that showed at the edge of the French rug. "A solid house," he said.

Miss Dove nodded. "A house built on sand," her heart whispered.

After Mr. Porter had gone she stood staring at the travel books. They seemed to mock her. It was for them that her father had ruined her life. She lay down, inert and hopeless, upon the horsehair sofa. She closed her eyes.

It was broad day when she opened them again. Slivers of sun slid between the closed slats of the blinds and were filtered through the Brussels lace curtains, and in Miss Dove's mind was the calm clarity of morning. A plan as clear and detailed as a well-drawn map unfolded before her. And that plan—that map of destiny—was illumined by a hard but happy truth. Nobody, not even her adored father, could ruin her life. Only she could do that. And she did not intend to.

She arose, bathed and dressed. Some impulse made her take her abundant hair in her two hands and twist it, so tightly that the skin was strained at her temples, into a knot. She walked downtown. When Mr. Porter arrived at his office he found her waiting for him. She looked so small and young in her mourning dress—so like a half-fledged blackbird—that she made his throat ache.

"Mr. Porter," she said, "I shall pay my father's debt." She looked directly at him, as if defying him to contradict her. "All I ask is time."

"My dear child—" said Mr. Porter. He took her gloved hand in his. Miss Dove withdrew it.

"We will keep the house and the books," she said.

29

"I shall secure a teaching position."

"You would ornament any profession," Mr. Porter said. "But what are you prepared to teach?"

"I know a good deal about the world," she said.

Mr. Porter made a benevolent clucking noise with his teeth. "I can scarcely imagine a young lady who knows less," he said gallantly.

The young Miss Dove's nose pinkened at the tip. She did not enjoy being patronized. "About the *Earth*," she said. "I have read my father's books. I shall teach geography."

The banker drummed his fingers. Though he was not a man who relished the prospect of turning widows and children into the cold, still he was far from rash with the stuff of commerce. But he saw something in the eyes of this redoubtable maiden that reassured him as to the safety of his money. "Suppose I make you a personal loan," he suggested. "I can reimburse the bank immediately, before there's any scandal. You can reimburse me at your leisure. Without interest."

"I am not asking favors," said Miss Dove.

"We can call this a favor to your father," he said. "He did more than one for me." For an instant he fancied he saw a bright film—a little dew of filial affection, perhaps—glaze the eyes of Miss Dove.

"Thank you," she said. "I accept your offer."

"Your father's only fault," Mr. Porter said with a catch in his voice, "was optimism. Remember that."

30

But some uncompromising accuracy within Miss Dove told her that she must recognize a fact for what it was. "He broke a rule," she said.

Mr. Porter escorted her to the door. He watched her thoughtfully as she walked away—back rigid, head high, glancing neither to the right nor the left. He went to the telephone and called the Superintendent of Schools.

The banker's recommendation did Miss Dove's project no harm, of course, and then the times were in her favor. Liberty Hill had long been affably incurious as to the world beyond its environs, but by 1916 the war in Europe had begun to trouble its composure. Vaguely, it felt that a vast portion of the earth that it had been wont to dismiss with the indifferent term "abroad" had become closer and more significant. It would be a splendid move—a modern, progressive move—thought the Superintendent of Schools, to secure a specialist in geography for the elementary grades. Besides, his wife was a third cousin to Mrs. Dove.

The rest of that summer, while generals mapped their strategies in France, Miss Dove mapped hers in her bed-chamber. To represent a classroom she laid her father's chessboard—an exquisite board of ebony inlaid with mother-of-pearl—on a table by the north window. The squares were desks. The ivory men were children. For hours on end, moving them about the board, speaking to them in unequivocal terms, she did what might be called "practice teaching." To the last detail she planned her procedure. The greeting to each class, as it entered the room ("Good Morning, Pawn," she said in a low, uninflected voice. "Good Morning, Castle. Good Morning, Knight."), the ceremony of its dismissal, the rules and penalties and forms were all settled upon. The presentation of her subject matter was carefully considered. And just as carefully, she considered how to impart the new and terrible knowledge that had come to her—life was not easy. Life did not excuse mistakes. Life demanded all the disciplined courage and more, that one could bring to it.

So, as she talked to the little carven figures on the board, she introduced moral value into factual matter. By slight variations of tone, compressions of the lips, or nods of approval, she made it plain that to her certain forces of nature, beasts of the jungle, and formations of the land were more worthy than others. She was partial to the yak which was "a useful animal"; she admired the domestic habits of bears and the cleanliness of cat creatures. Of ostriches who kicked, wolves who howled, monkeys who swung by their tails and chattered incessantly, she spoke with asperity. (The camel she gave his due. "He is not a pretty beast, either in looks or disposition," she told her class, "but he can go many days without water.") She

32

did not entirely approve of volcanoes: their action, she implied, was disruptive like the tantrum of a child. Rivers that overflowed their banks were rather silly. The grandeur of mountain ranges and the fertility of valleys she spoke of with respect. Her tone, when she described a plateau, was almost affectionate.

It was a game, of course—an absorbing game in which she forgot despair. But it was as serious as death—or life. It was the last game she ever played.

She had written the young archeologist that her bereavement would prevent her receiving him. If he had disregarded her letter—if he had come post-haste to Liberty Hill, stomped up the stairs to the bedroom, stormed the fortress, scattered the chessmen, clasped the young preceptress in his arms and loosened her bound hair—well, who knows? But he wrote Miss Dove a beautiful letter of condolence and kept his distance. He was not a Lochinvar.

In September Miss Dove exchanged her chessmen for pupils of flesh and blood. As she stood on the dais in the geography room, wearing her black mourning dress, her white handkerchief, and her small, tight, lustreless bun of hair, she looked very pale. But her pallor was that of purpose. She knew exactly how to proceed.

She kept her father's name clear of obloquy. She repaid Mr. Porter's loan, though that took twenty years. She saw that her sisters were suitably educated. She supplied her mother, through a long period of failing health, with every possible comfort and care and finally buried her with circumstance befitting a Dove of Liberty Hill.

In the accomplishment of these ends Miss Dove had denied herself much. She had ignored fashion. (Hair styles came and went—the spit curls, the overblown ear-puffs, the boyish bob, the page-boy, and the pony-tail. Flesh-colored georgette blouses were all the rage, knee-high skirts, empire waists, the New Look—she scarcely noticed them). She had dismissed her dreams of travel. She had renounced her youth. Persons of Mr. Porter's vintage who had seen her riding a blooded bay mare or standing in white beside her mother, winced at their recollections.

But Miss Dove did not wince. Fortitude—that quality of which her dear, weak father had spoken so often and so admiringly—sustained her and she discovered that responsibility was the native climate of her soul. She liked utilizing her strength to its utmost limits. She liked making and keeping rules. And just as a teacher with a genuine love for poetry will awaken that passion in her pupils, so Miss Dove imbued her charges with her philosophy. By her insistence upon even margins and correct posture and punctuality and industriousness, she told them, in effect, that though life was not easy, neither was it puzzling. You learned its unalterable laws. You respected them. You became equal to your task. Thus, you controlled your destiny.

Now, gazing at David Burnham she realized that she had gazed at him long enough. His mouth was beginning to tremble. She wished to rein his spirit, not to break it. With her map-pointer she gestured to the sink. "Very well, David," she said.

David went to the sink. He tore off a piece of paper towel, rubbed it on the bar of yellow soap, and scoured his mouth. He returned to the aisle.

"You may be seated," Miss Dove said. "Open your notebook to a blank page, please."

Miss Dove walked to the blackboard. Each step cost her an effort. It was as if her right leg had forgotten how to move of itself and had to be consciously directed. She took a stick of chalk and wrote a sentence on the board in her neat, round, legible hand. The chalk did not squeak. Chalk under Miss Dove's command never squeaked. She held it properly.

"Nothing is achieved by swearing," Miss Dove's sentence read. "Twenty times."

Twenty times was exactly right; when David had finished, the cafeteria would still be open. The supply of choice items on the menu—hot dogs and eskimo pies—would be exhausted, but he could nourish himself upon such less popular dishes as fish-loaf and tapioca pudding. It was Miss Dove's observation that whereas the punishment of a boy's palate had a salutary effect upon his behavior, the punishment of his stomach to the point of growling hunger often roused the brute in him.

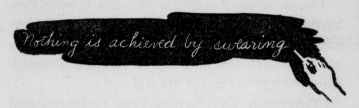

Nothing is achieved by swearing

She started back to her desk. She reached it just as pain gripped her in earnest. There was a crushing weight upon the lower part of her spine. A searing sensation flashed all the way down her right leg. A wave of giddiness swept over her.

She lowered herself into her chair. The pain lifted. But in its place was something more frightening than pain. In her leg, Miss Dove realized, there was no feeling at all. She pinched it to make sure. She tried to move it. It did not move.

For the first time since that evening in the shuttered parlor with Mr. Porter, panic seized her. She must do something. But what? She could send David for aid from other teachers but her heart sank as she imagined those women fluttering over her, exclaiming, witnessing the humiliation of her weakness. She wished,

36

above all, to behave with circumspection and aplomb.

"David," she said. Her voice was hoarse.

David looked up from his penance. He saw Miss Dove's face pasty-white—with anger, he presumed. He saw her hand gripping the map-pointer. He gulped. "Yes, Miss Dove," he said.

"Is your father likely to be at home?" she asked.

This was worse, thought David, infinitely worse than anything he'd feared. She meant not to beat him herself but to have his father do it, in her presence! He wished devoutly that he'd been content with a namby-pamby "heck" or "darn." He said nothing.

"Your father. Does he come home for lunch?" said Miss Dove.

Wildly David considered replying that his father had gone to New York or was in bed with pneumonia. But habit was strong. *He told the truth.*

"Yes, Miss Dove. Daddy's home," he said.

"I am indisposed, David," said Miss Dove. "I— Will you go and tell your father? Ask him to call young Dr. Hurley."

David could scarcely believe his luck. "Do I need a permission slip from the office?" he asked.

"No," said Miss Dove. "My permission is sufficient. Mention this to no one. And, David—" her tone came close to pleading, "do not loiter. *Run!*"

David ran.

Miss Dove noticed, with objective surprise, that she was trembling. Then, as she had before in times of transient trouble, she turned her mind to her work, which was eternal in character. She felt steady.

She stared critically at the second grade's mural. It was a jaunty effort, covering half the blackboard. It showed an expanse of snow, a row of igloos, a man, a dog and a reindeer (all approximately equal in size) and, in the background, the northern lights spreading a fan of garish colors—purple, green, orange, and pink. Across the white field of snow—lest anyone entertain a doubt—was written in large red script: The Artic.

The Artic

Reginald Smith had written that; Miss Dove knew his sprawling hand. Tomorrow she would call his attention to his error in spelling and have him write the word divided into its syllables—"arc-tic"—three times in his notebook.

But suppose she were not here tomorrow? Suppose

38

—the palms of her hands grew clammy—she were never here again. Rubbish! That was arrant nonsense. Except when the school itself had been closed because of blizzards or epidemics or a burst boiler, she had always been here. She was not entirely proof against the ills of the flesh, but she managed to suffer them at convenient times. Miss Dove had her colds during the Christmas holidays. She had summer complaint in the *summer*.

The pain had been mechanical, she decided. A kink in a muscle. A sudden movement of a joint held stiff too long. And the numbness? But why should numbness be alarming? Feet went to sleep and woke again. Soon young Dr. Hurley would arrive. He would prescribe a tonic and a heating-pad. He would warn her, in the coarse, jesting way that she would accept from nobody else, that the ideal of perfectionism was repugnant to God and man—that she ought to kick up her heels, raise merry hell, go on a three days' spree!

Dr. Hurley was seventy-two. It was to distinguish him from his doctor-father who had delivered her and had been dead now for a quarter-century that Miss Dove called him "young." In his actual youth he had been a radical—doubting the efficacy of the calomel purge and scoffing at the theory that the blood grew thick in winter—but, to the general astonishment, he had not killed his patients. And the years had mellowed him. Beneath his bluster he was, Miss Dove felt, a sound man. She trusted him.

"A penny for your thoughts, Miss Dove!"

Lorraine Ellwood, the music teacher, stood in the doorway. She was a wispy blonde of thirty-four who had begun to fade without knowing it in the crumply way of a hothouse rosebud. She wore bangs and an Alice-blue dress with a dirndl skirt that had come from a sub-deb shop. She was fond of saying that she felt like a big sister to her pupils and although her devotion to them was sincere—Miss Dove granted her that—she could not control them because she lived on their level. She had, Miss Dove thought, more soul than sense.

"Mona Leckford's engagement is out of the bag," she chirped. "We're cutting a cake in her honor in the rest-room. Won't you join us?"

Miss Dove indicated the essay papers. "Thank you, Miss Ellwood," she said. (She remembered her colleague as an infant in a go-cart, but while on duty she did not use first names). "Unfortunately, I am busy."

"All work and no play—" Lorraine began and let her voice trail off without finishing the proverb.

"Be so kind as to convey my felicitations to Miss Leckford," said Miss Dove.

"We'll miss you," said the music teacher as she turned away. Her little feet went down the hall, pittypat, like the feet of a dainty child.

Suppose, Miss Dove thought, letting her mind return to its hideous speculations, the doctor didn't pooh-pooh her complaint. If she were really ill, if her strange bodily sensations declared the close of her career as the buzzer had declared the close of the morning's work—*what kind of teacher would take her place in the geography room?*

Would it be a soft little person like Lorraine Ellwood? A person who did not guess that children must be marshaled and trained for life as green soldiers are trained in field manoeuvres for the reality of battle? A person who lived in a never-never land where discipline was a singing-game?

Would it be a brash hearty girl like the art teacher? Someone who encouraged self expression? (Miss Dove had seen paintings done in the art class—great, free, brilliant blobs of color running into the margins, and had shuddered to imagine maps executed with such techniques!) Someone who shouted for order and grew red in the face?

Or worst of all—oh, too bad to think of!—would another Mona Leckford sit here on this dais, slumping, stifling yawns behind a hand? A languid woman, Miss Dove thought with contempt. A teacher *whose heart was not in her work!*

Suddenly the room seemed thronged with figures. They folded their hands and waited for Miss Dove to direct them.

She leaned forward.

41

Let happen what may, she promised silently to the phantom company, *I shall return!*

There was a sound of footsteps—rapid, solid, masculine—in the hall. The Reverend Alexander Burnham hurried into the room. With him was Dr. Thomas Baker. David brought up the rear.

"Davie said you needed help, Miss Dove," said Alexander. "So I brought Tommy."

"Young Dr. Hurley is my physician," said Miss Dove. Her tone implied that to ask for a seasoned medical man and to be offered instead, the services of Thomas Baker, was like being sent a troop of Boy Scouts when one had requested aid from the militia.

"Davie told us that," Thomas said quickly, remembering the importance Miss Dove had always attached to the delivery of "a straight message." He felt protective toward David and, illogically, toward himself. The familiar room was casting its spell upon him. The mural on one blackboard, the map on the other, the clay caribou on the sand table, the cactus plants on the window sill and, above all, the dry odor of chalk and boy that permeated the air (chalk smells the same forever and so do little boys, he thought with a sense of discovery)—all these belied the passage of time. He was eight years old, or eleven, or twelve at the most. He was facing the terrible Miss Dove who had accurately surmised, through some clairvoyance of her own, that he had a live garter snake in his trousers pocket. "Dr. Hurley is ill with a recurrence of his

42

bronchitis."

"The immoderate use of tobacco," Miss Dove said. She glanced at David who was guilty, she suspected, of smoking in the boys' basement.

David slid into his seat and resumed his copy-work.

"Quite likely. At any rate, he's *hors de combat*," said Thomas. (He was surprised and somewhat elated at the formality of his own language.) "I happened to be at Sandy's when David came."

"Tommy's had excellent training, you know," said Alexander.

"I know," said Miss Dove. Of course she knew. It was she who had begun his training. It was she who, day after unremitting day, had drilled into him respect for industry, desire for exactitude, and the civilizing grace of inhibition. "Only—" Only what? Only that for all his six-foot stature, his degrees, and his accomplishments, he was still, to her, the boy who had wiggled his ears whenever her back was turned.

Thomas understood Miss Dove's hesitation. He remained near the doorway, standing firmly upon etiquette. "Perhaps Miss Dove would prefer someone riper," he said.

But Miss Dove was not prepared to wound an old pupil's professional pride. Besides, she needed advice.

"I shall be glad of your opinion, Doctor," she said. With succinctness and clarity, as though she were listing the chief products of the Great Lakes region, she described the symptoms of her malaise.

43

Thomas nodded. He strode across the floor. He mounted the low, raised platform (and as he did, he had the feeling that he took the final and necessary step up from childhood to the plateau of adult authority); with the tip of his finger he touched a spot in the teacher's rigid back.

Sharply, Miss Dove drew in her breath.

"That's all," Thomas said. "Was it bad?"

"Yes," said Miss Dove.

"I was afraid it would be," Thomas said. "And your leg? There's a complete absence of sensation?"

"My limb has gone to sleep," Miss Dove said. "As soon as I move about—"

"But that's what we can't allow," said Thomas.

"Can't—what?" Miss Dove inquired. It had been a long time since anyone had proposed to impose his will upon her.

"Can't allow you to move about," said Thomas.

"And pray who are we?" Miss Dove asked with acidity. She glanced at Alexander Burnham. Her glance was a challenge.

Alexander fiddled with his clerical collar. "This isn't my province," he said. "Tommy's the doctor."

"Lindbergh's 'we,'" said Thomas. "Me. I—that is."

"What is your diagnosis?" asked Miss Dove.

"I haven't one yet," Thomas told her. "I'll have to get you to the hospital. Right away."

"Is that necessary?" Miss Dove demurred. "Young Dr. Hurley—"

44

"It is quite necessary," Thomas said. "Right away."

"Next week, perhaps," said Miss Dove. By next week Dr. Hurley's bronchial tubes would doubtless be clear and his comfortable skill at her command. "At present I am very busy. I am reviewing my grammar grades for the state proficiency tests. They will be given on Monday."

"Right away," said Thomas. His voice was flat. In it was the unyielding tone she had heard in her own when her patience was tried and she meant to brook no more nonsense.

"But the fifth grade is weak on the winds and the tides," she said.

" 'There is a tide in the affairs of men—' " said Thomas. "Frankly, Miss Dove, the decision is not yours. Medicine is *my* theater of command."

"Yes, Thomas," Miss Dove said meekly.

"Shall I call an ambulance?" asked Alexander.

"No! Please!" begged Miss Dove. With horror she imagined a siren shrieking down the street. She saw herself supine on a stretcher emerging from the portals of Cedar Grove School. "Not an ambulance!"

"I know," said Thomas. And he did know. In his instant of power he was granted perception. "Sandy and I could carry you to my car. That won't be so comfortable, of course—"

"It will be quieter," said Miss Dove. "More discreet."

"Very well then," Thomas said briskly. He wished

to seize, before it changed, Miss Dove's submissive mood. "Now, Sandy—"

"My hat, please," said Miss Dove. "My gloves and my bag. They are in the closet."

"I'll fetch them," said Alexander. But with his hand on the china knob of the closet door he trembled. He was about to penetrate an awful mystery. How often, especially when his conscience had been heavy, he had looked at that closet door and looked away! No one, to his knowledge—no one except the terrible Miss Dove—had ever seen behind it. Speculation had been rife, of course, and everyone had agreed that the closet was an eerie place festooned with cobwebs and containing strange instruments of torture. There were rumors of blood stains on the floor. One lad with a ghoulish literary bent (he had later become a successful playwright) had claimed to know for a certainty that the skeleton of a boy was propped, grinning, against the wall. The children didn't really believe in those Gothic fancies, of course, any more than they believed in other dreadful rumors—that ghosts walked on Friday nights, for instance; that they, themselves, would some day lie in the graveyard; or that Miss Dove chastized miscreants with her map-pointer. They clung to them because they gilded dull routine with danger. Alexander opened the door.

The shallow, white-washed closet was uncluttered. From a peg beside the door hung a turkey-feather duster. On the floor were a pair of rubber gaiters and

standing in the corner was no fleshless cadaver but a furled umbrella. From a shelf Alexander took Miss Dove's hat—black, small, straight-brimmed, a hat and nothing more—her long gold hatpin, her gray gloves, and her handbag. He backed out of the closet shutting the door quickly lest his son David should see inside and suffer disillusion.

Miss Dove drew the gloves over her long, elegant fingers. In one hand she took her hat, in the other, her pin.

Alexander averted his eyes. (It had been the consensus of his classmates that the teacher secured her hat by driving that pin straight through her cranium.) His gaze met Thomas' and asked a question.

Thomas answered with a shrug. His expression was grave.

Miss Dove's hat sat, level and steady, upon her head. She looped the strap of her bag over her arm.

"I await your convenience, gentlemen," she said.

"If you'll lean forward—this way," Thomas said, helping her to her feet, "and support yourself on the desk— Now, Sandy!"

The two men joined their four hands, making the sort of chair that children make at play. They lowered it behind Miss Dove.

"Sit down," said Thomas. "Put your arms around our necks."

All this while David had bent over his notebook, intent on escaping notice. But when he heard the doctor's strange command and realized to whom it was addressed, he looked up. His marrow was chilled.

His father and Dr. Baker had lifted Miss Dove into the air. She was sitting between them, on their hands, with her bony arms (and how, David wondered, could they endure the touch?) hugging their necks. Her feet dangled down.

"You may go, David," she said.

"Yes, Miss Dove," said David.

Alexander regarded his son. "Were you kept in because of your conduct?"

"Yes, sir," said David.

Alexander glanced at the board. His face darkened the way—David remembered—it had darkened at breakfast. "Have you finished your twenty copies?"

"I've done fifteen," said David.

"Do the other five," said Alexander. "Do five extra for good measure."

Miss Dove stiffened. This was the typical parental error. To indulge a child in his folly, gloss over his faults and then, in an outraged moment, to punish him excessively.

"David has been diligent," she said. "He was interrupted to run an errand at my request."

"He has to learn—" David's father began.

"It is I who deal with him here," said Miss Dove. "To borrow Thomas' words, this classroom is *my* theatre of command. David may go."

"Yes, Miss Dove," said Alexander. He and Thomas carried their proud passenger into the hall.

Left alone, David began to weep. He wept because, being a child of sensibility, he appreciated the austere beauty of justice and was moved when a tyrant came to his defense. He wept because he sensed that the world was subject to change and because to be left to his own undirected devices made him feel forlorn. He hated himself for crying. He hated his tender nature. It was his dream to become a big-league pitcher or a space-rocket pilot like the heroes on the ready-to-eat cereal boxes—who were *never* pictured in tears!

"Hell and damn!" he said aloud to the echoing room.

But the fine-flavored oath had lost its tonic property.

It caused him to feel no bigger, no tougher, no less deserted. Why, he thought, shocked at the heresy to boyhood, the teacher was right! Nothing *was* achieved by swearing.

Nothing is achieved by swearing

Down the central corridor of Cedar Grove School Miss Dove was borne aloft. The big front door was open to the brilliant day; the corridor was dim by contrast, like the tunneled passage in a dream. The pictures on the walls—those reproductions in sepia of Galahad petting his horse, of Washington kneeling in the snow, and of the peasant girl enraptured by her lark, all of which had been chosen for moral inspiration —looked blurred and shadowy and downright silly. The drinking fountain, a fixture of which Miss Dove severely disapproved (she regarded it as an open invitation, like a poolroom, to laxness and rowdy behavior) had an aspect of pathos. From the teachers' rest-room on the second floor came Lorraine Ellwood's thin, true voice singing "Always" in honor of Mona Leckford; it sounded wistful and unreal—the ghost of a song. Yes, everything was very strange. And strangest of all was the fact that Miss Dove, herself, should move without the exercise of volition through territory where her presence had stood for law.

"Spine straight, Miss Dove," Thomas warned her. "Don't wobble about."

Miss Dove could scarcely believe her ears.

"It is not my custom to wobble," she said.

They approached the door. Beyond lay the school-yard—a piece of the large, uncloistered world—harsh with the glare of publicity. What would the children do when they saw her? Would they stare? Would they gape? (Miss Dove abhorred a hang-jawed child!) Would they giggle? She did not know. She only knew that children in the mass were unpredictable.

But she must face them, and face them down. She thought of the Spartan boy smiling while the fox gnawed his vitals (though he had been *wrong* to steal the fox in the first place—she had always reminded her pupils of that); she thought of Marie Antoinette on her way to the guillotine. Then, as if she were recall-ing another figure from history, she saw the young girl she, herself, had been. She saw that girl lifting her head above dismay; twisting her pale, bright hair—the symbol of everything easy and debonair—into a hard knot; bending above a chessboard by a northern win-dow. *I* am predictable, she thought.

Alexander Burnham glanced up at her briefly. His brown eyes, remarkably like David's, were full of con-cern. "You'll be all right, Miss Dove," he said.

"I am always all right," said Miss Dove.

Mercifully, although she was prepared to carry it off with eclat, Miss Dove was not obliged to run the gauntlet of her pupils. A soft-ball game and two or three vendettas had drawn the student body to the playground behind the school. On the front lawn only a flock of robins and one child, hidden among the boughs of the namesake cedar, observed Miss Dove's departure.

The robins cocked their yellow eyes and continued pecking for worms.

The invisible child was Vicky Evans, the dreamer. She had climbed the tree for solitude. She was thinking up a story. And just as the elements of literature— an explorer lost among the mountains of the moon, a ruined castle, an enchanted princess—had begun to emanate from her mind, she saw something stranger than fiction. She saw two tall men carrying a woman between them. The woman was Miss Dove. There was no mistaking, even from a distance and through the gloom of the cedar, the prim black hat and the handkerchief-flower on the bodice of the dark dress.

In her first surprise Vicky felt only a mild shock of
the ineffable wonder that all children feel when events
go topsy-turvy. It was the way she might have felt if
she'd heard a white rabbit talking to himself or seen
a baby turning into a pig. But as she watched the

53

group move down the cement path through the schoolyard, she was seized by horror. Miss Dove was being abducted! She had been "drugged into submission"—that was why she did not scream!

The fact that Vicky recognized both the "abductors"—that Mr. Burnham was the rector of her church and Dr. Baker the surgeon who had removed her grandmother's gall-bladder—did nothing to allay her fears. (She had learned from comic books that wolves employ many disguises other than the fleece of lambs.) Swinging from limb down to limb, like one of those arboreal monkeys Miss Dove disliked, she dropped to the grass. She raced across the lawn, scattering robins.

She plunged through the doorway and ran, with mounting terror, down the cavernous hall of the school. Her voice froze in her throat. When she saw five or six teachers descending the stairway, looking gay and sentimental, she began to howl.

"Vicky, darling!" cried Miss Ellwood, rushing ahead of her companions. "Are you hurt, dear?"

Vicky shook her head. Between howls she made a burbling, unsuccessful attempt at articulation.

"Something's frightened her," Mona Leckford said, with an air of perspicacity.

"Steady in the boat there, Evans!" boomed the art teacher.

"Kidnappers!" Vicky managed to gasp. "They've snatched Miss Dove!"

The music teacher sat down upon the bottom step

54

and pulled Vicky into her lap. "Sweetheart," she said, "you've been making up stories—nice little let's-pretend stories that belong in books and you're all mixed up. But we mustn't confuse let's-pretend with really-so, must we?"

"They snatched her!" Vicky sobbed. "I saw them!"

"Classic hysteria," said Mona Leckford who dipped widely, if not deeply, into the literature of abnormal psychology. She peered at Vicky. For the first time in her brief teaching career she found a child fascinating.

"It's her vivid imagination," said Lorraine. "Now, Vicky-Wicky, let's think hard! You didn't *see* them. You just—"

Then David Burnham came out of the geography room and told what had happened.

Miss Dove was not transferred to the doctor's automobile. Thomas decided against that for fear of jolting his patient. He discussed his decision, beneath and across Miss Dove, with Alexander.

55

"It's five blocks to the hospital," he said. "Can you make it, Sandy?"

"If you can," Alexander replied. He sounded offended, as though he considered the question a reflection upon his age (he was a few years the senior of Thomas) or upon the staying power of the clergy.

"Good man," said Thomas.

"What of Miss Dove's comfort?"

"Oh, she'll be okay so long as she keeps her spine rigid," Thomas assured him. "And that's an old habit of hers."

Miss Dove found it odd to hear herself spoken of in the third person as if she were absent or deaf. Odder yet, it was agreeable. For the fact that she was not consulted put her anxieties—for a brief interlude at least—at a certain remove. Like any pupil in the geography room she had now to think only of her present duty and that duty was defined. *She was to keep her spine rigid.*

Back down the route she had taken in the morning she rode between her bearers. Along Maple through a shower of winged, coral-colored seeds some of which settled on her hat; up Oakwood, across LaFayette, past her own house to Elm where, half a block further on, the hospital was situated.

The noonday hush was on Liberty Hill but Miss Dove's progress did not go unnoticed. Polly Burnham was on her porch, awaiting her husband's return. She started forward when she saw him; he warned her off

56

with a shake of his head. He walked very slowly, she observed, keeping careful step with Thomas. She telephoned Jincey Baker.

Jincey called her sister and her mother-in-law. Within five minutes a score of persons stood, half-eager and half-afraid, at front windows. And when they beheld the awaited spectacle they felt betrayed as people feel when they first glimpse the outrageous fact that their parents are not immune to change but have been touched, as by frost in the night, with an intimation of mortality. If Miss Dove's strength could crumble, what of their own? The shape of bones showed through the buxom face of nature—

Law, embodied in the muscular bulk of Patrolman Holloway, was cruising the streets in a police car. The car drew close to the curb.

"Has there been an accident, Doc? Is she bad off?" Holloway asked. He was abjectly devoted to Miss Dove who had once shown him consequence when that was what he needed. He pronounced "she" as with a capital letter, like the pronoun of deity.

"I have the immediate situation under control, Bill," Thomas said. "Scoot over to the hospital and tell them I want a private room. Say I'm not asking for it—I'm *telling* them!"

"Yes, sir." With siren wailing, the car sped off at sixty miles an hour.

Jincey Baker was in her front yard. She wore a full yellow smock. The sun gave an extra gloss to her hair.

57

Her complexion had the glowing delicacy that blesses some women in the terminal weeks of pregnancy and there was a sprinkling of freckles—a touching, left-over grace of childhood—on the bridge of her exquisite nose. She looked like Spring.

After nearly a year of marriage, Thomas was not hardened to his wife's beauty. For an instant the world rocked and he was oblivious of all else. He nearly stumbled.

But Miss Dove was not dazed. She noted only that the girl seemed to have outgrown the flighty butterfly airs that had made her first youth absurd.

"How d'y'do, Virginia," she said.

"How d'y'do, Miss Dove," said Jincey. She looked at her husband. "Can I help, Tommy?"

"No," Thomas said. He rapped out the negative, wishing to cut clear of the tenderness that threatened to unman him. "Just look after yourself. Don't do anything foolish."

Silently, Miss Dove approved the doctor's admonition to his wife. His tone had been unnecessarily brusque, perhaps—but what better advice could a man give Virginia (who had been one of the volatile Webbs) than a warning against impulsive behavior?

It had been nearly a year before—the very first day of the preceding June, to be exact—when Miss Dove had talked alone with Jincey in the geography room, had been interrupted by Thomas, and had been reasonably sure, when she'd seen the two young people go off together, of how the next chapter of their lives would read.

That first of June had been graduation day at Cedar Grove Elementary School. The exercises had not deviated from tradition. On the platform of the school auditorium forty white-clad children of the outgoing sixth grade, all with rapt, dedicated faces, had presented a tableau of propriety. (At least thirty-nine of them had. Sterling Baker, a boy remarkable for pinkness and aplomb, had attempted, by practicing Morse code with his mobile ears, to provide comic relief for the transcendent solemnity of the occasion. But, with a single exception, the audience had ignored Sterling. Only his elder brother, Dr. Thomas Baker—the sole visiting adult male in attendance—had suffered a brief fit of coughing.) "Trees" had been recited with much flutter of the hands to denote nesting robins, much walling of the eyes to denote piety, by Fae Patricia Rigsbee, a bisque doll of a girl. Finally, the Citizenship Cup had been awarded to Lester Knight, Jr.; thrusting his lower jaw forward almost to the angle of dislocation, Lester had declared that to him the trophy "rep-er-esented just one more challenge!"

At last the graduates left the stage. Preceded by the

59

principal and most of the faculty, they marched single file down the center aisle of the auditorium. Their voices, raised in the school's song of farewell, had a sweetness independent of pitch or harmony.

"Dear old Cedar Grove, to thee-ee-eee
We pledge love and loyaltee-ee-eee—"

sang the graduates and proceeded to vow, off-key, that whatever temptations might beset them "upon life's stormy sea" (i.e., junior high school) they would cling to the ideals of their first alma mater. Every mother who heard them (even the rare candid one who considered her own darling's eligibility for promotion a minor miracle) grew damp in the eye.

Miss Dove was acquainted with the sensibility of the female parent. On thirty-odd successive Commencement Days, just at this point in the ceremonies, she had been aware of an increased humidity in the emotional atmosphere. And, since she had taught most of the mothers present and knew their individual quirks, she could—if pressed—have told what each of them thought in her heart or whispered to her neighbor.

"They will become the men and women of tomorrow," murmured Lester Knight, Junior's mother. Like her son, she had a gift for appropriate platitude.

Mrs. Rigsbee, sandwiched between Mrs. Knight and her own young sister, Jincey Webb, suppressed a sneer. "What does anyone expect them to become? Yaks?"

60

she inquired behind her hand of Jincey. It was obvious to Mrs. Rigsbee that except for some foul element of favoritism her Fae Patricia would have received the cup.

Jincey shrugged. *What dull, provincial lives these women lead,* she thought. *Never tasting glory or despair. Moving about in their little orbits from market to P. T. A. to country club to market. Merely motorized vegetables.* She raised her lovely eyes to the ceiling. *At least I have suffered. I have lived!*

At the tail end of the line, separated by three paces from the last singing child, came Miss Dove. She walked with her usual measured tread. She wore her usual dark dress. She looked precisely as she had always looked. But she knew that the mothers, regarding her through a haze of emotion, saw her with a difference. Ordinarily—try as they might to disguise the fact by poking fun at her sharp nose, her impassive countenance, and the tight little ball of hair at the nape of her rigid neck—they were afraid of her. "The terrible Miss Dove," they had called her in their childhood and still called her; and their title for her derived less from her dogmatic insistence upon the less dramatic virtues than from the suspicion that she knew all about them. She could put her finger on the snively, ignoble spots in their natures as unerringly, they felt, as she could touch with her long map-pointer the capital of Bolivia or the source of the Danube. But on this June morning most of them forgot that.

Rich and charitable in successful maternity they glimpsed infinite pathos in the spinster's life.

She was no longer the terror who had stalked through their school days—who had made them wash out their mouths when they'd chewed their pigtails or used inelegant language; who had forced them, through dread of her silent contempt, to sit still until the bell rang, no matter how badly they needed to go to the bathroom; who had known, though she hadn't stooped to question their word, when they were fibbing. She was not even the cold-blooded monster who had, later, remained unsoftened by their own children's infantile graces—by Sistie's bashfulness and Bubbie's imperfect articulation, and the adorable way Jackie Boy stomped his foot, like a regular little man, when his will was crossed. She was Woman Bereft.

For the sixth-graders were leaving her. Each one irreplaceable and differing from all other children as star differed from star, they were marching straight out of her life as sixth-graders had marched, June after June, year after cruel year. They would never return.

"Poor Miss Dove!" the mothers sighed in silent unison and Miss Dove heard them with that inward ear, sensitive to vibrations of the mass mind, that is the genius—though scarcely the bliss—of the true teacher. "Poor childless, chickless, figless Miss Dove!" The sentiment drew them together into one warm, yeasty lump of compassion. Forgiving the miscarriage of the Cup, Mrs. Rigsbee reached for Mrs. Knight's hand

and squeezed it. Very tenderly she laid her other hand over Jincey's.

Jincey withdrew her fingers. She lifted her head in a delicate, fastidious way as if to hold it aloof from banality. On her pale face was the languid hauteur that is natural to a young beauty whom tragedy has touched.

Miss Dove, though she was attempting to notice nothing, noticed Jincey. It would have been difficult not to see the slightest motion of the girl's head with its red-gold hair that seemed to give off sparks like a cat's fur stroked in the dark. Miss Dove noticed, as well, that Thomas Baker noticed and that his eyes appeared dazed as if they were staring into an open fire.

Miss Dove was not pleased. She was cognizant of the details of Jincey Webb's disappointment. She could imagine (though she could *not* imagine allowing herself to wander into such a predicament) that to be publicly jilted was galling to the self-esteem. But she gave short shrift to the wan weeds of melancholy. If Virginia—for Miss Dove believed in calling people as well as facts by their full names—would stop mooning about in an atmosphere of broken orange-blossoms, play-acting and walling her eyes much as her silly niece, Fae Patricia, walled hers, then she might reap some benefit from experience and enjoy a fuller, saner life.

As for Thomas Baker—surely a qualified surgeon, accustomed to the stern realities of health and sickness, could keep his mind from meandering in the maze of a girl's red hair. Surely he must realize—as Miss Dove realized—that those distracting tresses had done Virginia harm. If her mother had kept them braided, the nonsense of beauty and glamor would never have begun. (Miss Dove reflected complacently upon her own hair—washed once a week, brushed night and morning, and screwed into a sensible bun out of folly's way.) And if Thomas wished to contemplate something other than his profession he might well consider the flippant attitude—that sad family failing!—that his young brother had just displayed upon the rostrum.

But disdain as she might the marvelous hair and the bemused, half-drowning look in the doctor's eyes, Miss Dove was not oppressed by them as she was by her consciousness of the sticky emotion that oozed toward her from the assembled matrons. Her place in society was one, Miss Dove believed, to excite envy. That other women should presume to pity her—and especially that soft species of women who leaned upon the protection of men and who, with the advent of maternity, lost the power of reason and replaced it with a vague, yearning sort of mawkishness that they held sacred and called instinct—seemed to her fantastic. She was not tempted to laugh, for a sense of humor was not her defense against impudence. That touted faculty she regarded, indeed, as morally vestigial and, like the tonsils, apt to breed trouble. She looked through air as clear as glass upon the human scene; in it she saw much that was right, much that was wrong, and nothing that was funny. No. Laughter was not her style. She was inclined, however, for one outraged instant, to come to a full stop in the aisle. To stand there, revolving slowly like a weathercock on a windless day, sweeping her sympathizers with a gelid gaze that would leave them little doubt as to her opinion of mothers.

Naturally, however, the sedate Miss Dove did not yield to that impulse. She continued her stately progress as rear guard of the graduates. The position was not—as the lachrymose mothers thought—one of loneliness or rejection. It was a position of her own choosing. Seven years before a disconcerting thing had happened at a Cedar Grove graduation. The last child in the line—a little girl known as Jincey whose angelic brow and pellucid hair had moved most people to poetry—had whipped a water-pistol from the depths of her frilly bodice and had shot the boy preceding her in the seat of his trousers. Other guns had appeared as if by prearranged signal. The graduates had broken ranks. They had rioted through the building, leaping desks, drenching flowery-bonneted bystanders with the ammunition of their side-arms and singing, instead of the school's inspiring anthem, a rowdy ballad known as Pistol-Packing Mama! Since that unhappy day, Miss Dove had deemed it prudent to let the children know that the eyes of decorum were upon them, aft as well as fore.

Now, nineteen and wretched, Jincey herself recalled that occasion. She smiled, remembering the surge of daring, the intoxicated leap toward freedom. And she remembered as well, the disciplined years that had, paradoxically, given her the heady moment of bravado. Miss Dove did not evoke her pity. Jincey saw her as the symbol of a bygone era when life had been unchancey and as plain as a map on a wall. She remembered how the teacher had stood, stiff as a yardstick, behind her desk; with her long fingers she had touched the globe of the earth, turning it slowly to illustrate its predictable diurnal revolution. And, recollecting, Jincey experienced again an old, comfortable conviction that if you obeyed the law—if you sneezed in your handkerchief and raised your hand for permission to speak and kept your margins neat—that globe and all it represented was certain to be your oyster.

For the first time in weeks it occurred to Jincey that a broken heart was cumbersome baggage.

Miss Dove followed the class into the hall. The mothers arose. They fanned themselves with their programs. "It was the end of something," they said mournfully, "but think—now we'll have our families all to ourselves, all day, all summer!" Then, staring suddenly down a tunnel of ninety hot, unbroken days of intensive maternity, they added, as if to bolster their optimism, "Poor, dear Miss Dove!"

"It's nice to see you here, Jincey. It will mean so much to Little Fae," Mrs. Knight said. "That green dress with your hair—" Her glance was caressing as behooved a glance cast by a fruitful married woman upon a slip of a girl whose hopes were blighted, but it was patronizing, too. Lester, Senior, was no Romeo, the glance said. He didn't own a yacht. His Adam's apple was prominent, he snored, and his jokes were ancient. But he had *been* there when he'd said he would—waiting at the altar!

"She came to please me. She's a cutie-pie," Mrs. Rigsbee said, giving her sister an affectionate spank. "We're driving out to the club for lunch. Afterwards you can get a swim and a sunbath, Jince. I put your things in the car."

Jincey felt smothered by tact and solicitude. And to be called "a cutie-pie" was more than she could bear. "I believe I won't. Thanks all the same," she said. She added, and the resolve, and the words that clothed it were simultaneous, "I want to go see Miss Dove."

Before her sister could argue she escaped and went her way.

"Hi, Ellen. Hi, Jane," said Dr. Thomas Baker to Mesdames Knight and Rigsbee. "This makes me feel my age and more. You two girls here *in parentis* and me *in loco!*"

"Wasn't it sad?" said Mrs. Knight. "I bawled at the song. And poor Miss Dove!"

"*Poor?*" Thomas demanded. "She scared me stiff the way she always did. I sat there sweating—perspiring I mean—and wondering if I had a clean handkerchief." He took a handkerchief from his pocket—it was quite clean—and mopped his brow. "No. She'll always be 'the terrible' to me and nothing more!"

"But she's old, Tommy," pleaded Mrs. Rigsbee. "And lonely. Year after year other people's children leave her forever!"

Thomas thought he could endure with equanimity a lifetime minus the company of the affected Fae Patricia, the pompous Lester, Junior, his own ebullient sibling, Sterling, or any other twelve-year-old. But he did not voice his unorthodox sentiment. He was, after all, a young physician with his way to make. "Wasn't little Jincey with you?" he asked, employing an elaborately casual tone. "I hadn't seen her since she was Fae's age, but I spotted that fire-engine hair."

"She *was* here. It's the first time I've been able to drag her out since—" Mrs. Rigsbee finished with a

68

wave of her hand. "She went off to speak to Miss Dove."

"A palpable error," Thomas said. "She could have waited and spoken to *me*." He raised his left eyebrow in the cocksure, maddening, irresistible manner of the skittish bachelor who doesn't underestimate his value. He drifted with the crowd to the door.

Back in the classroom—her castle, as it were—Miss Dove sat at her desk on the dais and closed her eyes. Below her, five rows of lesser desks stood tenantless. The blackboards were washed clean of drawings of isthmuses and peninsulas. The sand-tables were shrouded in oilcloth. But Miss Dove was not closing her eyes against the sadness of these things. She was trying to visualize clearly the twoscore children who had left her. For six years she had pruned and polished and molded them and had sought to blow into their clay the breath of purpose. Now they had passed beyond the scope of her influence, beyond the aid of her stricture or approval. She did not wish them back. She wished only to believe that they would do well without her. But she had to wait and see. Miss Dove was like an author whose book was on the press, like a cook whose cake was in the oven, like a flight instructor whose cadet had departed on a lonely mission in the sky. For weal or woe her job was done.

But as the author ponders the merits of that poetic passage in his third chapter, as the cook wishes she had flavored her batter with almond instead of vanilla, as the instructor wonders about forced landings, so Miss Dove tormented herself with questions. She thought first of Fae Patricia. The child was tractable and honest but she had given herself a great many airs today as she'd recited Kilmer's poem. *Did I teach her enough humility? Enough common sense to withstand the adulation of a fatuous mother and many fatuous men?* Miss Dove thought, with a pang, of Fae's aunt, Jincey Webb.

Jincey had been a likely child. Not intellectual or original, but thoroughly nice—cheerful, obliging, and amenable to suggestion. Though she had been subject to animal spirits (witness the "pistol-packing" episode) she had recognized the beauty of discipline. Her notebooks had been jewels of neatness, things of sheer delight. And her posture had been superb—spine straight, head erect, feet planted on the floor. And then, within a few years of her leaving Cedar Grove, something had happened to the girl. Everything about her—her complexion, her figure, her direct brown eyes and, most demonstrably, her hair—had taken on a kind of burnished symmetry that had dazzled the beholder. Worse, it had dazzled Jincey. At the State University she had been elected—by acclaim —the "Sweetheart of Sigma Chi." She had won a talent show and had gone to New York where she got a small job singing TV commercials for a shampoo product—though her voice was slight and indifferent

70

in quality. Soon her engagement had been announced. She was to marry the scion of a wealthy family. She would have a Mediterranean honeymoon aboard a private yacht. She would live, when she returned, in a penthouse—a twelve room cottage with a terrace and a lily pool built in the sky above Manhattan.

She had come home for the wedding. She had wanted it in the little stone church where she'd been christened with all her old friends there to bless her.

But the wedding had been a mirage. Two days after Jincey had arrived home her fiance had eloped with a night-club entertainer. He had not apprised Jincey of his intention. She had heard of it, as a *fait accompli*, on a radio gossip program.

Miss Dove had not been greatly astonished by the turn of events. She had seen a photograph of the defaulting groom and had noted a shiftiness in his eye and an over-fullness, indicative of petulance, about his mouth. What *had* astonished her had been Jincey's behavior. The girl had not conducted herself with the poise that should have distinguished an alumnus of Cedar Grove. She had wept and wilted. She had secluded herself in her sister's house where she had allowed close friends to dab her forehead with *eau de cologne*. She had not—though Miss Dove would have phrased the matter with more urbanity—had the guts to spit in the eye of circumstance!

Was there something more I could have done, Miss Dove asked herself now, *before the girl was twelve?*

She sighed and considered the case of Sterling Baker. It was odd and discouraging how an idiosyncracy could run like a warped thread through a whole family. Sterling was the youngest of four brothers. Thomas, Andrew, Randolph, and Sterling—Miss Dove had taught them all. They all had cleft chins. They all had fine muscular control—they could wiggle their ears; they could raise one eyebrow without so much as twitching its mate. They were all quick to learn and respond to ethical values. None of them knew how to lie. But try as she had, Miss Dove had never been able to cure them of their love of clowning. And of course she'd got no help from their mother. "Oh, they'll be serious soon enough," that fat, amiable woman was reported to have said. "Leave them to fate and the terrible Miss Dove!"

Recalling Mrs. Baker's remark, Miss Dove pursed her mouth as though she held pins in it.

There was a hesitant step at the open doorway. Jincey Webb stood on the threshold. "Good morning, Miss Dove," she said. Her voice was that of a well-instructed child. It made her unchildish beauty seem fancy dress put on for a masquerade.

"Good morning, Virginia," said Miss Dove.

Jincey advanced into the room. Her shoes were thin green shells supported by thin, high heels. Her green

frock made a sound reminiscent of wind in grass.
Her hair shook off a peculiarly unacademic fragrance.
Jincey went straight to the third seat in the third row
of desks.

"This was my place," she said.

"Will you sit there now, Virginia?" Miss Dove said
politely.

Jincey took her seat. "The room is different,
empty," she said.

Miss Dove was not adept at small talk.

Jincey made another try. "Like life," she said.

Miss Dove said nothing.

"It doesn't smell the same, either," Jincey said.

73

"Remember the boys' corduroy pants—dirty and sort of cheesy at the end of the week? And wet sneakers?"

Miss Dove maintained her silence. To discuss odors, especially in reference to persons or clothing, she considered coarse.

"Is that the same map?" Jincey asked. She pointed to the large map of the world that hung, rolled up for the summer, above the blackboard behind Miss Dove. "Is China still orange?"

"It is a new map," Miss Dove said. "China is purple."

"I liked the old map," Jincey said. "I liked the old world."

"Cartography is a fluid art," said Miss Dove.

With the flat of her hand Jincey pushed her hair back from her forehead. She had done that in moments of perplexity long ago. "Oh, Miss Dove," she said, and her voice shook, "tell me what to do!"

Miss Dove was not at a loss. She told Jincey in three short words. "Do your duty," she said.

Jincey's eyes filled with tears. "But what is your duty when your world has ended?"

"You are nineteen, I believe," said Miss Dove. Her statement was devoid of sarcasm. Miss Dove had been nineteen when her own world had ended and begun. And now she could remember without pain or longing the old lost world. It was a charming memory, like a fairy tale read to a sleepy child. But the new world was real. Whether she was happy in it she did not ask herself. She was strong. She was useful. She was Miss Dove.

"This is how it was," Jincey said. She told Miss Dove all that had happened to her. None of it was wicked. All of it, as Miss Dove had surmised, was a chronicle of vanity and innocence. She told of meeting Michael, the villain of the piece, at the Stork

Club. "He spoke to the waiter in French," she said, "and wore a cummerbund."

She told of the places he had taken her to dine. "Did you ever drink champagne, Miss Dove?" she asked.

"No," said Miss Dove.

"It tastes like cider," Jincey said, "but its effect is different." She told of the compliments Michael had paid her. She told of his proposal. ("You are my rainbow's end," he had said.) She was on the verge of describing the sensations she had experienced when he'd clasped her in his arms, but at that point Miss Dove halted her.

"Reticence, Virginia, is the sine qua non of gentility," Miss Dove said.

Then Jincey told of the evening in her sister's house when the devastating news had come over the radio. "Everything went black," she said. Tears gushed down her cheeks. She looked very appealing, not very pretty, and about ten years old. "Next day I had a telegram. It said, 'Gorgeous, only you can understand.'"

"Could you?" asked Miss Dove.

"No," Jincey sobbed. "I still can't. Can you?"

"Certainly," said Miss Dove. "Have you a handkerchief, Virginia?"

"I forgot," said Jincey.

From a box on her desk, Miss Dove took a piece of facial tissue. Like a queen stepping down from her throne to distribute largess to the poor, she stepped down from her dais and gave the tissue to Jincey. She returned to her desk.

Jincey wiped her eyes. She blew her nose. "What must I do—exactly?" she asked. She folded her hands and waited to be told.

Of course Miss Dove knew the answer. Jincey's problem, like most problems, was uncomplicated when viewed objectively. And yet, she hesitated. To tell an adult exactly what steps to take toward his salvation was apt to weaken him. It deprived him of his inalienable right to trial and error which was tonic to the character. But today Jincey laid the claims of childhood upon her. She was sitting in her old place. And she had forgotten her handkerchief.

"Very well," Miss Dove said quietly. "First, you must return to your sister's house. You must enter your bedroom, fall upon your knees, and give thanks to your Heavenly Father."

"Thanks!" Jincey gasped. "For what?"

"For preserving you from a fate worse than death," Miss Dove said. The expression, uttered in her precise, calm accents, sounded neither trite nor melodramatic.

"Than death?" Jincey echoed.

"Than death," Miss Dove repeated flatly. "It is evident that the young man to whom you had given your affection discovered that his feelings for you had altered."

Jincey nodded, dumb with misery.

"He had, however, an honorable avenue of escape. He could have requested you to release him from his commitment."

Jincey began to cry again.

"He did not choose to take that honorable avenue," Miss Dove said. "Why?"

"I don't know," said Jincey.

"Then I will tell you," said Miss Dove. Her tone was bland and informative. She might have been explaining the difference between longitude and latitude. "It was because he was a cad, a coward and a person of low principles."

"Oh!" cried Jincey. She sounded shocked, as if she were hearing blasphemy. But slowly over her face spread an expression of exquisite relief. "I thought there must be something wrong with *me!*"

"Your fault lay in a rashness of judgment," said Miss Dove. "His lay in dishonor." She paused to let the distinction sink into the girl's consciousness. "And then," she went on more briskly, "after you have expressed gratitude to the Power that kept you from a disastrous alliance, you must consider your duty to your neighbor and yourself. You must find a useful occupation."

"Do you think I could teach?" asked Jincey.

"Decidedly not," said Miss Dove. "But there are other spheres of service."

"I might be a nurse."

"You might," Miss Dove agreed. Nurses were disciplined. They wore uniforms. Their shoes had low, solid heels. And their hair! Miss Dove thought approvingly of Jincey's hair tucked into a net and crowned with a starched white cap.

"I might enter a nursing order," Jincey said dreamily, "and become a nun." She laid her hand, in a graceful gesture of renunciation, upon her bosom.

"What's this about nunneries?" Thomas Baker demanded from the doorway. He sounded alarmed and breathless, like a doctor who hopes he's arrived in time to countermand a wrong prescription.

"Good morning, Thomas," said Miss Dove.

"Good morning, Miss Dove," said Thomas. He came into the room, a tall, lean young man with a humorous mouth, a steady eye and a stubborn chin. "Why, Jincey!" he exclaimed, affecting surprise at her presence. "Holy mackerel, kitten, you're all grown up!" His tone implied that fact to be felicitous and arranged primarily for his benefit.

"So are you," said Jincey.

"Naturally," said Thomas. He was twenty-nine. He had fought in a war and studied medicine and was on the staff of the local hospital. Of course he was grown up. "But it's rather odd of *you*. Though extremely becoming."

"Thank you," said Jincey. "It's nice you approve."

"The last time I saw her was before I went east to med school," Thomas told Miss Dove. "I was being separated from the Navy and she from Cedar Grove. She shot my brother Randy in the—"

"Virgina cannot enjoy being reminded of that," said Miss Dove.

"It was very reprehensible," Thomas said. "You must be relieved, Miss Dove, to be finished with us Bakers. Sterling was mamma's last black lamb."

"Sterling has many sterling qualities," Miss Dove

79

said with no intention of making a pun. "Except for his levity—"

"Levity is a handicap," Thomas said. "I'm a martyr to it. I often think it's what's kept me single. I'm going fine with a girl, you know. Everything's leading up to Lohengrin. And then—just at the throbbing, tender moment—I can't resist a wisecrack!"

Jincey laughed. Her laughter was sweet bells in tune. She tossed her head. The dazed expression passed over Thomas' eyes.

"Sterling's behavior during the graduation was inexcusable," said Miss Dove.

"He was giving me the SOS with ear jerks while Fae was reciting Trees," said Thomas. "I taught him to do that."

"It was rude," said Miss Dove.

"I'll speak to my mother when she returns from Boston," Thomas said. "She knows how to deal with smart guys."

"I dare say," said Miss Dove.

Jincey wrinkled her shapely nose. "Does this room smell different to you, Tommy?"

Thomas took a step toward her. He inhaled deeply. "And much better," he said.

Jincey laughed again.

Miss Dove deplored what seemed to be transpiring before her eyes. Jincey's new found purpose was not yet proof against blandishment. In the Webbs the vein of romance ran as close to the skin as did the vein of comedy in the Bakers.

"I expect the hospital keeps you busy, Thomas," she said.

"Yes. It calls me now." He glanced at Jincey. "My car's out back. If I could drop you off somewhere—"

"Fine," said Jincey. She rose. "Good-by, Miss Dove. And thank you. I'll remember." (But it struck Miss Dove that she'd forgotten a good deal already.) "I'll think about the nursing career. Maybe Tommy can advise me."

"I'll advise her very carefully," Thomas said with the utmost gravity. And suddenly, just before he left with Jincey, he gave Miss Dove a smile of such ineffable sweetness as she had never seen before. She remembered a metaphor, read somewhere long ago and scarcely thought of since, that spoke of life—or was it love?—as "honey on the tongue."

Miss Dove put on her hat without benefit of mirror. She closed the windows and drew the green shades down over the glass. In the dim, watery light the room looked mysterious, like a room in a dream. For an instant Miss Dove had a fleeting vision of children—familiar children and yet new—stirring in the shadows. All the end-of-the-year fatigue fell away from her. She felt elated and greedy for the future. It was a curious sensation. Perhaps it was what people meant by happiness.

I am fifty-four, she thought. *I won't have to retire until sixty-seven.* She paused, calculating. (A different kind of woman would have counted on her fingers.) If they didn't tarry—and recalling the smile and the laughter, she didn't expect they *would* tarry—then she could take the first child straight through to graduation.

The child would need her. Jincey would be a doting, dandling mother. She would rock her children to sleep and kiss their bruises and call them by baby-talk names like Punkin and Buttons and Boo. And Thomas, as a father, would cut a sorry figure indeed. Fancy a father who was a "martyr to levity." A father who "couldn't resist a wisecrack!"

And yet, Miss Dove reflected, possibly all that, along with shiny hair and silly shoes and pretty smells (for Jincey's agreeable scent still hung on the air), was part of a plan designed by an Authority she did not question. For if everyone lived upon Miss Dove's own lofty plane—if everyone perceived with perfect clarity the hard, serious truths of human life—then there would be no parents and no children. There would be only teachers.

In this magnanimous mood Miss Dove left her classroom. In the foyer of the building, under the picture of Galahad and his horse, the art teacher had set up a trestle table and was serving refreshments to the graduates and their guests. Miss Dove moved among the

82

mothers, greeting them graciously. As she approached Mrs. Knight she saw that lady slap a slice of coconut cake out of the hand of her illustrious son.

"Lester, Junior, you pig!" Mrs. Knight sputtered between clenched teeth. "You're going to be sick, sick, sick, and serve you right!"

"Good morning, Mrs. Knight," said Miss Dove. "I'm sure you are proud of Lester."

Mrs. Knight wheeled around. With her foot she shoved the cake, which had fallen to the floor, beneath the overhang of the crepe-paper tablecloth. As she gazed up into the teacher's serene, cloudless, omniscient eyes—as she imagined a summer uncluttered with the care and feeding of children—pity was the least of her emotions.

But she managed to compose her features. She put her arm around Lester, Junior's shoulders. "All that he is he owes to you, Miss Dove," she said.

Miss Dove inclined her head in acknowledgment of the tribute. "It is my rule," she said, "to regard my each success simply as one more challenge."

And now, from the elevation of the crisscrossed hands of Burnham and Baker, Miss Dove looked down at Virginia and saw that she—against the odds of soft hair and eyes, pretty bodily proportions and a heart

83

very quickly made glad—had attained, no less than Lester, Junior, the condition of being "a challenge." In the gauzy April light she stood there in her husband's garden—still beautiful and still, perhaps, a trifle too conscious of her beauty, but with all her folly fallen away. She carried her unborn child high, as the country saying is, and she carried it with pride. In her face was the steady glow of vocation. Maternity, Miss Dove felt, was a humbler career than teaching—a talent rather than a craft, drawing more from instinct than from intelligence. But it was abundantly clear that it was this girl's—this woman's—ordained sphere of usefulness, that she had found it and that she would give it her energies without reserve. That was success; Miss Dove respected it. It gave her the same stab of esthetic satisfaction that she had often felt when some hitherto graceless child had shown understanding or had made a map with meticulous care (preventing the colors of different nations from running into one another), or had told the truth when the truth was to his immediate disadvantage.

When they came in view of Miss Dove's own house —a large white house, with fluted columns and a cut-glass fanlight, that had long since been converted into apartments—Miss Dove suggested stopping while she gathered together a few conveniences.

"No," said Thomas.

"I'll attend to them later," the minister said.

"I am afraid that is an office for a lady," said Miss

Dove.

Alexander blushed. "Most certainly," he said. The notion of invading Miss Dove's virginal boudoir, of touching her comb, her toothbrush, and her various articles of intimate apparel, caused his nerves to quiver. "Polly will get them."

"We're almost there," said Thomas as he and his companion turned into Elm Street.

"If I may be permitted to indulge my curiosity," said Miss Dove with a touch of hauteur, "how long must I expect to be hospitalized? Overnight?"

"Longer than that," said Thomas.

"This is Wednesday," said Miss Dove. "I should like to be in school by Monday at the latest." She could give the children no factual aid on their tests, but she could aid them intangibly merely by being there. In her sedative presence they would be unlikely to be rattled.

"Not next Monday," said Thomas. "A week from then maybe. Or a month. It all depends."

"Oh," said Miss Dove.

In the front bedroom of the bungalow that abutted the hospital grounds John Wesley Evans had just arisen from his couch. Wes, as he was known generally, was a man of charm and unfortunate habits. He was recovering from a spree of considerable scope so—and what could be more natural?—he poured himself a little "hair of the dog." He took his glass to the window and raised it in a salute to a new day and a new start. Light kindled in the liquor. Fire, he thought, in the heart of a rare jewel. He was smiling, somewhat fatuously, at his pretty conceit when he saw Miss Dove.

The sight unnerved him. Several times before he had been subject to alcoholic fancies, but those had taken vague, fumey shapes suggesting snakes and legendary beasts. He had never seen anything like this.

"Come here, Pearl," he implored his wife who was entering the room to bring him a raw egg masked in Worcestershire sauce. "Quick!"

Pearl hurried to his side. "Why, it's Miss Dove," she cried. "Your terrible Miss Dove!"

"You see her, too?" Wes said. His forehead was damp with the sweat of relief. "But what else do you see? Who's got her?"

"Tommy and Sandy," Pearl said. "She must be sick."

"She must be more than sick," said Wes. The teacher's face—a tragic mask, he thought, put on for death—moved him deeply. He differed in many salient respects from Miss Dove, but he admired her. What she stood for—certitude, principle, authority—was what Wes yearned to stand for. Often it was the ap-

86

palling consciousness of the gulf between the ideal and the reality that sent him to the bottle.

" 'The time you won your town the race

'They chaired you through the market place—' " he quoted softly.

"What say, darling?" his wife said in an anxious tone.

"Housman," he said. He set his glass down, untasted. "I'm through with *that*, forever!"

"Of course you are," Pearl said as she had said countless times. She did not know what passed through his mind (after all, she had been raised in another town), but she knew that something had touched a liberating spring in his nature. For weeks now—oh, for months with any luck—she could bask in the halcyon weather of her husband's sobriety. "Can you swallow an egg?"

Absently, Wes swallowed the egg.

He continued to stare out the window. He could now see only Miss Dove's back—the prim feet visible beneath the decent skirt, the uncompromising neck, the shape of the hat as stiff and uncoquettish as a mortar-board. But upon his mind her pale set face was stamped. The nose was supercilious. The brow was lofty and calm. The eyes met with recognition, he was sure, with composure and cold disdain, the eyes of mankind's uncouth and dusty foe.

However, as had happened before, his poetic temperament deceived him. Miss Dove was not thinking of death. She was thinking of the proficiency tests.

But the hospital, like the theatre or the school-room, is a world contained in itself, turning on its own axis. In its atmosphere is some hypnotic or amnesiac quality before which ordinary life recedes. Even Miss Dove, with her high resistance to foreign influences, was affected by the spell. She approved of the hos-pital. Of its formality, its regard for order, and its implacable determination to seem exactly what it was. The faint pervading odors of ether, lysol, and formal-dehyde did not offend her; they were germane to the place as the odors of chalk, floor-oil, and children were germane to a school building. She admired the way the nurses walked—briskly, without switching—with their starched skirts making a clean, rustling sound. She admired the way they did their hair (they wore it tucked into nets and topped by stiff caps that were only by accident more ornamental than her own black hat) and the way they all had fluted handkerchiefs peeping out from their breast pockets, and the way they stood at attention and said "Sir" in the presence of doctors. She admired—though with initial reluctance—the authority exercised over herself.

She did not, of course, quite abandon her self-determination; she relinquished it into temporary safekeeping along with two possessions of value that she carried in her purse. One was a mother-of-pearl cardcase containing a dozen visiting cards upon which her name (plain MISS DOVE without amplification) was engraved in chaste block letters. The other was a large, heavy-lidded gold watch that had been her father's. In this place she had no need to prove her identity (it was posted on the outside of her door) nor to measure the passage of time. She lay becalmed in the present.

When Mr. Spivey, the principal of Cedar Grove School, called to express his concern for her health and to say he was assuming personal responsibility for her classes (he would be up at the bat pinch-hitting for her, he said, for he was an idealist who thought of life as a major sport) he found her curiously at ease. Not once did she fix him with the dead-sea gaze that had so often made him feel naive in faculty meetings. Even when she touched upon the preparation for the coming tests—upon the fifth grade's confusion about the winds and the tides, for instance—she seemed neither tense nor haughty. Next day, with a catch in his voice, he told his teaching staff: "The old quarterback is resting on her oars!"

(Like many men who employ athletic metaphor,

89

Mr. Spivey leaned to the potpourri.)

The hospital, forewarned by Holloway, had been ready for Miss Dove. It was small by contemporary standards but big for Liberty Hill and so new that its vanity was still intact. When word came that the town's perfectionist was bound thither, everyone, from the superintendent down, rose to the challenge.

The double entrance doors were flung wide. Against one of them stood the superintendent himself. (He had been, Miss Dove recalled, a boy who organized his time.) Against the other stood William Holloway. They stood at attention as if awaiting a visit of state. As she passed between them Miss Dove bowed graciously, once to the right and once to the left.

Inside the lobby, near the door, was a bed made up with linen that shone like snow against the moss-green walls. Beside it stood a thin, black-haired nurse.

So gently that she felt only a twinge, Miss Dove was deposited upon the bed. She looked up at solicitous faces. It was a new sensation for her who was accustomed to look down at faces from an eminence.

"I secured a special in case you wanted one," the superintendent said. "A 'practical' was the most I could do for day duty, but Mrs. Green is one of our best."

"I try to be," the nurse said, drawing a blanket over Miss Dove's knees. "Do you remember me? I was Billie Jean McVay."

"Yes," said Miss Dove. She remembered Billie Jean

very well. A sloe-eyed child who had been languorous at seven and who, at twelve, had troubled the air of the school with a suggestion—almost an aroma—of sex precociously in the ascendant. "I remember you, Mrs. Green."

"Of course, I'm older now," Billie Jean said as if she'd read her patient's thoughts.

Alexander took his leave and Thomas, after a hurried consultation with the nurse, did likewise. There was an emergency case for him, the superintendent told him. The Knight boy—Lester, Junior,—had been admitted half an hour before with abdominal pain and a high white count. His mother was with him, in worse shape than Lester.

"I daresay," said Miss Dove. She could imagine how Jane Knight would behave under threat of a son's appendicitis. (Jane had been a Simpson. All Simpsons were flighty and likely to go to pieces on examinations.)

Thomas, who was also acquainted with the Simpson strain, laughed shortly. But immediately he sobered. He felt himself projected into the future and had a vision of Jincey distraught beside a suffering child— running her lovely fingers through her lovely hair and praying God to let the doctor come. "I'll see you later, Miss Dove," he said. He walked rapidly away without a backward glance.

Miss Dove did not feel abandoned. Thomas, she knew, had put her problems into the proper pigeon-hole of his mind, much as she did with the problems of the third grade when the fourth grade trooped in.

"I'll take you up now," said Billie Jean. The bed was on rollers. Grasping it by the footboard she propelled it down the hall to the elevator.

Miss Dove had traversed that hall before but as a visitor, under her own power, and in an upright position. Now, with the power gone and the position changed, that hall, like the hall of Cedar Grove School, seemed different and longer.

The nurse's skirts made a whispering noise—like water among reeds, she thought—, the light had an aqueous quality, and she, herself, seemed to be drifting in a boat. The fancy produced in her a rhythmic peacefulness, as of lapping waves, and the rhythm became a recollection. She remembered a parody in verse that one of her less reverent pupils had composed back in the '30s.

Geoffrey Lyons the parodist had been. (A fat boy with a sullen, and even stupid-looking countenance that had a disconcerting way of lighting up suddenly, for no discernible reason.) He had taken for his model some lines from the Arthurian legends—those elegiac lines describing the "lily maid," the fair and lovable Elaine. "Miss Dove the grim, Miss Dove the terrible," Geoffrey had written. "Miss Dove the Gorgon's Head of Cedar Grove!"

Some tattle-tale prig had left the verses on Miss Dove's desk hoping, no doubt, to anger the teacher and make trouble for the poet. But the prig had failed on both counts. Miss Dove's concept of honor would not have allowed her to be affected by an anonymous communication. Besides, she would have stooped to anger with a twelve-year-old boy no more than she would have raised her voice or bribed her class to good behavior or reduced learning to the level of entertainment. When, twenty years later, Geoffrey had become a playwright of distinction, she had been mildly elated and not particularly surprised.

At Geoffrey's invitation she had condescended to be his guest at his first play's opening night. He had sent her an orchid and a round-trip ticket on the plane to New York. And Miss Dove, though she hadn't flown before, had felt entirely comfortable as the huge airliner bore her above a terrain with whose contours she was, academically speaking, familiar. (She took the precaution to sit far front where she could, if it seemed expedient, advise the pilot in matters of navigation.) She had been comfortable in the theatre, too. Geoffrey's play, dealing as it did with the problems of three marines who were stranded upon a tropic isle among a number of hibiscus-clad female natives, struck her as lacking a certain elevation of tone, but it did not embarrass her. Nothing embarrassed Miss Dove. After the show she boarded the one-o'clock plane for home so as to avoid being late for school next morning.

Later, when school was over, she had written a letter. "My dear Geoffrey," she wrote in her discreet, legible script, "As your former teacher, I am gratified by your worldly success. But in the same capacity I am obliged to recommend to you the cultivation of felicity in language. With more than three hundred thousand words at your disposal in any unabridged dictionary, is it necessary to permit your characters the use of expressions that are frequently inelegant, often profane, and (unless I misinterpret their meaning) occasionally improper?" Before she made her signature she hesitated. An odd light—something very like a twinkle—appeared in her eyes for a moment. She signed herself "The T. Miss D."

Gossip columns reported that when Geoffrey read the letter, sitting with a bunch of his cronies at Toots Shor's, he wept aloud and implored God to make him a better man. But Miss Dove had never credited that story. She'd thought it unlikely that any of her "old children"—even those who dabbled in the creative arts —could so far forsake the principles of dignity and restraint.

Now, in her illusory floating state, as Geoffrey's audacious lines recurred to her, she suddenly perceived a connection beyond the metrical between herself and the lady from Astolot. Elaine had floated, too. Elaine had floated upon a bier. Is this bed—? Am I—?

The unfinished question was preposterous. She lifted a hand as if to banish it into limbo.

"Are you feeling ill, Miss Dove?" asked Billie Jean.

"I was thinking of Lord Tennyson," said Miss Dove.

"Oh," said Billie Jean. "That's nice." She was not at home with the Victorian poets but she felt safe in the choice of her adjective. Whoever or whatever Miss Dove thought of was bound to be nice.

The room into which Miss Dove was wheeled was a small, blue room. Its window, giving upon budding treetops and gabled roofs, was like a big framed picture that dwarfed the wall.

"Now we'll take off our clothes and then we'll feel more comfy," said Billie Jean. She spoke in a humoring tone with steel behind it. It was clear that she intended to assume command.

"The pronoun 'we' is misleading," said Miss Dove. "Unless you propose to take *your* clothes off."

Billie Jean tittered nervously, but refused to be intimidated.

She undressed Miss Dove. ("You're not to try and help," she said. "Dr. Baker doesn't wish you to exert yourself.") She removed Miss Dove's outer garments, her camisole and chemise and petticoat and her old-fashioned boned stays. She gave her a bath.

"I made my ablutions this morning," demurred Miss Dove.

"It's routine," Billie Jean said, lathering her patient's flat, immaculate stomach.

"Very well, Mrs. Green," said Miss Dove. She could not, in conscience, oppose routine.

"Now here's something to make our skin soft and sweet. *Your* skin," Billie Jean said. She smoothed a few drops of emollient lotion over Miss Dove's neck and shoulders. "Know what I think of when I put this on my patients? The little can of talcum you gave me for Christmas in the third grade."

"The second grade," said Miss Dove. Her Christmas gifts had long been standardized. Talcum was for second-grade girls. Girls in the third grade got celluloid thimbles.

"Mine had a picture of lilacs on the tin," the nurse said. She eased Miss Dove's arms into the sleeves of a cambric bed-shirt.

"Yes," said Miss Dove.

"I was some kind of proud," said Billie Jean. She pulled the bed-clothes up. "And when you gave it to me you said something I never forgot. You said: 'This is to use *after* you wash your neck.' "

"I intended no reflection upon you," Miss Dove said quickly. "That is what I say to all the little girls."

"I didn't take it personal," Billie Jean assured her. "But it's funny what kids remember. I can hear you say that like it was ten minutes ago!" She emptied the bathwater down the lavatory drain and hung the washcloth and towel (neatly, Miss Dove observed, with the corners pulled out straight) on a rod. She returned,

96

still talking, to the bedside. "You know how some girls can't pass a cosmetic counter without they spray themselves with free cologne? Well, I couldn't bring myself to do that. I'd feel dirty. Everybody thinks it's so queer!"

"Our standards are our own," said Miss Dove. She was, she discovered, fatigued. She wished that hospital regulations enjoined silence upon nurses—that they were required to raise their hands for permission to speak.

But it was Miss Dove's lips that were closed. Billie Jean stuck a thermometer between them.

"It's not that I don't care for perfume," she mused on after a minute of grateful silence during which she had counted her patient's pulse. "I guess every normal girl does. Take my baby—my little Ava. She's going on five and she's crazy about my Elizabeth Arden's 'Blue Grass.'" She withdrew the thermometer. "But I tell her every single time she begs for it—I say: 'First, you go wash yourself good!'"

"*Well*," murmured Miss Dove.

Billie Jean, mistaking the monosyllabic correction for an exclamation of interest, nodded. "That's exactly what I tell her!" She read the thermometer and jotted down a figure on a small pad.

"What is my temperature?" asked Miss Dove.

"That's confidential information for the doctors," said Billie Jean. Apologetically, she patted Miss Dove's hand. "Even if I told you, you wouldn't know

97

what it meant. It's in centigrade."

Miss Dove did not defend herself against the girl's bland assumption of her ignorance. "My question was indiscreet," she said.

"Oh, no! Not indiscreet!" Billie Jean protested. "All patients ask. But you know rules."

"Yes. I know rules," said Miss Dove.

"That 'Blue Grass,'" Billie Jean said, as if eager to return to a safe subject. "Bill Holloway gave it to me. He said it smelled refined." She blushed shyly. "He's going to give me something else. A ring."

"An engagement ring?" asked Miss Dove.

Billie Jean nodded. "I feel like a dream walking! I've been a widow for five lonely years and now—"

Miss Dove made an inarticulate sound of sympathy. Billie Jean, she knew, had gone west to work in a factory. She had been married there to a Mr. Green who had met with some sort of untimely—and, perhaps, unseemly—demise, the details of which had never been clarified in Liberty Hill. At any rate, Billie Jean had returned with a new name and a new baby and had become a practical nurse.

"And now," sighed Billie Jean, "I'm the happiest girl in the world!"

"But your life is full as it is," said Miss Dove. "You have your child and your work."

"A woman's life," said Billie Jean, "is never too full for a man!"

Miss Dove said nothing.

"Bill has you on a pedestal," Billie Jean went on. "He says you're his idea of 'genteel.'"

"I value William Holloway's opinion," said Miss Dove.

She voiced no idle politeness. She did value his opinion as she valued her own. That fact would have startled the society of Liberty Hill in which Miss Dove was considered—not entirely without reason—to be something of a snob. But such snobbery as she had was not of the common variety that flies, like a homing pigeon, to money or prestige. She was a moral snob. And so, in his way, was William.

Anything could be taught, of course—fine points of deportment as well as the names of the tributaries of the Nile. By six years of drill and example—forty-five minutes a day, Monday through Friday, September through May—Miss Dove had brought many a child to conform to a code that ran counter to his inclinations. But now and then—oh, a dozen times, perhaps, in the course of her teaching career—she had met a child in whom the ethical instinct, microcosmic but fully-formed, was as innate as original sin. It was an almost mystical thing, that gift for goodness—and rarer than mathematical genius or perfect pitch. Hardened as she was to surprises, Miss Dove never recognized it without a sudden leap of the pulse. She had recognized it in William.

All the signs had been against the boy. He came from a home—if one could call it a home—that might

99

euphemistically have been described as "underprivileged." He was an orphan who lived with his grandmother, a woman of unsavory repute, in a leaky shack near the gas-works. On his first day at school he had been barefoot. There had been scabs on his toes. His hair had been matted and over one pasty cheek had been the brownish stain of a fading bruise. He had held an elbow crooked as if to ward off a blow.

Mothers, entering their pretty six-year-olds in Cedar Grove School, had gasped. One, a Mrs. Holmes, had begged Miss Dove to keep her son on the other side of the room from William.

"I believe in democracy," she had said, "but I don't want Charlie to catch anything!"

"My seating arrangement is alphabetical," Miss

Dove had told her coldly. But privately her heart had sunk.

It was wearisome enough to deal with raw but scrubbed first-graders from decent families. An unwashed child from the criminal fringe of town posed a problem indeed.

And then William surprised her.

All the rules of manners and procedure that Miss Dove persuaded ("bullied," her critics said) the other children to accept, William took to his bosom. When he greeted Miss Dove at the door he did so in the accents of dedication. At her "attention please" he sat up straight and showed the proud poker-face of a soldier presenting arms. He began to wash. Like a badge of honor he wore a clean handkerchief protruding from his breast pocket.

Miss Dove gave him Saturday jobs raking leaves or mowing grass. He performed these jobs well and later, on her recommendation, he procured a paper route. He was the best paper boy in town. He was never late and he always laid the paper, folded, on the doorstep instead of twisting it and tossing it on the roof. ("What is worth doing is worth doing well," Miss Dove had said and William had taken her literally.)

Shortly before he finished the sixth grade Miss Dove had put beside his name in an old leather-bound ledger a single letter that was her mark of unqualified approval.

The ledger in which Miss Dove made that mark

was no ordinary roll-book containing a record of pupils' attendance and statutory misconduct. It was a book as sacrosanct as that golden one in which Abu Ben Adam's angel wrote in the lily-like room. No human eye except Miss Dove's (and that eye, there were many to say, was something more or less than human) ever perused its pages. In it were inscribed the names of all the children who had passed, during Miss Dove's incumbency there, through the final grade of Cedar Grove School. In it each child was given a single letter of the alphabet indicating what Miss Dove considered the basic trait of its character. (Miss Dove generally thought of children as "its" instead of "he's" and "she's.") She could have guessed that trait, with fair accuracy, the day any child first came into the geography room frightened or boisterous or homesick for its mother. But, in charity, she deferred her judgment. Unpromising as any lump of humanity might be, there was always the possibility that half a dozen years of thumping and molding might work it into respectable shape. Not until Miss Dove was nearly done with a child, until it was about to escape forever from her supervision, was she willing to call its character established.

The commonest letter in the ledger was T for Tract-able. That letter was appropriate for the rank and file of Miss Dove's pupils—youngsters not born for Who's Who but amenable to reason and capable, under wise leadership, of becoming decent citizens. There were a number of W's for Willing given to those children who showed more than the usual desire to be improved. There were some A's for Awkward and a sprinkling of B's—a really bad mark—which stood for Babyish and was given most frequently to the kind of pouting little girl who would become, in the future, a fattish middle-aged woman who wore frilly bathing-suits that showed her stomach and wept when the cook failed to come. O's for Original went to unregu-

lated children who formed ideas of their own without consulting Miss Dove, who decorated their maps with pictures of Viking ships off the coast of Denmark, or were disposed to argue points of philosophy. (O's were not signs of Miss Dove's esteem; she gave them

regretfully. She had given one to Geoffrey Lyons.) But beside William Holloway's name she placed the symbol that she might, without undue complacency or spurious modesty, have placed beside her own. It was an S. It stood for Satisfactory.

And yet, highly as she had regarded him, she had known far less of him outside the geography room than she had known of most of the children. For though it was her custom to pay pastoral calls at the residences of her pupils, she had never called upon William's grandmother. In his case, she had felt a separation of school and home to be eminently desirable.

So she never saw the squalid little house on the alley until William had been for years beyond her care. And then it wore a pitiful dignity. Upon its door was a sheaf of carnations. It was a house made significant for a day by death.

In a larger world than that of Cedar Grove, beset by temptations and not sustained by the classic simplicity of inflexible rights and wrongs, William had not done well. He had played truant. He had hung around pool-rooms. Once he had been haled into juvenile court for shooting crap. And yet Miss Dove had not lost faith in him. The thing that set him apart from the generality—a congenital sensitivity to virtue— was, she believed, enduring. As a diamond dissolved in the crucible hardened again into its pristine chrystalline shape, so William, with any modicum of luck, would return to his S. She would have liked to help ensure that luck. But what could she do? She was a teacher, not a probation officer.

One day, when William was seventeen and had quit school, Miss Dove heard that his grandmother was dead. She had died under sordid circumstances. In a free-for-all fight over the rights to a debouchment of coins from a slot machine, someone had split her skull with a beer-bottle. She was to be buried late that afternoon.

After school Miss Dove put on her hat and gloves and set out for the house of bereavement. On the listing lean-to porch were a few neighbors. Miss Dove bowed distantly to them. She walked straight to the door.

Inside, wearing an ill-fitting, evidently borrowed dark suit, stood William. He was a tall fellow now—thin, but with powerful shoulders—and Miss Dove thought she had never seen a more perplexed distress than that which marked his face. (It was like a bruise—the bruise he had worn on his first day at school.) She extended her hand.

"May I offer my expressions of sympathy?" she asked.

William took her hand. He straightened his shoulders. "Thank you, Miss Dove," he said. "Would you like to come in and see Grandma?"

There was little Miss Dove would have liked less, but she followed William into the front room. There the remains of the disreputable Mrs. Holloway reposed in a cheap coffin. In death, Miss Dove was certain, the old woman had achieved an aspect of decency that she had not achieved in life.

"She did the best she could," said William. "She didn't—" he gave Miss Dove a glance of reverence. "She didn't have my opportunities."

"Her troubles are over," said Miss Dove.

"I hope so," said William. "Some say they're not."

Miss Dove rode with William to the cemetery, sitting erect in the undertaker's limousine. But when the obsequies were over she bade him farewell. "I will walk home," she explained. "I wish the exercise."

Then she looked William full in the face and said in a clear tone that could be heard by all the lesser mourners, "I shall follow your career with interest."

She went off, leaving him to decide in that loneliness which is the true climate of decision, whether to respect his life or throw it away.

As it turned out, William was sensible. He joined the army. After three years, honorably discharged and seventy pounds heavier, he returned to Liberty Hill. Using his G. I. educational allowance for living expenses, he completed his high-school education. Then, with a sound understanding of himself, he entered the field of law enforcement.

Each morning when Miss Dove saw him at the intersection of Grant and Maple—spruce and solid, lifting his great, white-gloved hand to halt traffic or beckon children across the street—she experienced a moment of stern exhilaration. There was a man whose mind and muscles functioned in harmony. A man in love with his work. For him, she knew, a policeman's lot was a very happy one.

Of his domestic lot, which he planned to cast with Billie Jean's, Miss Dove was less certain. And yet, she remembered, Billie Jean *did* wash her neck before applying scent. That was a straw in the wind.

"I've tired you," Billie Jean said ruefully. "I always go yak-yak when I'm nervous. You see, Bill thinking so much of you and you being the terri—well, being who you are—I got flustered."

"That was natural," said Miss Dove.

"A nurse has got no business being natural," said Billie Jean, rebuking herself. "A nurse should think of her patient."

Quiet reigned in the room. Miss Dove relaxed. Some thread that had always stretched taut, holding her fast to responsibility, seemed to have snapped clean through. She closed her eyes and let her mind bob up and down like a cork on the surface of a pond. She thought of pleasant, far-off things. Of a golden afternoon when she had sat on a campus lawn with the young archeologist, watching cloud shadows move over the grass and talking of the buried cities of antiquity. Of her mother arranging roses in a silver bowl. Of her little sisters wishing on the first star. Of her father reading aloud by the fire. And often, as those images thinned out like smoke, she did not think at all.

Billie Jean fed her soup from a spoon. A technician drew blood from her finger-tip and carried it away in a test-tube. She scarcely noticed.

Through the window floated the blithe and quarrelsome voices of children released from school. They floated from an alien sphere, from a point remote in time.

An interne came into the room. He was a short young man with a crew-cut, bright pink cheeks, and the gloss of appalling youth. In his white coat and trousers he reminded Miss Dove of a sixth-grader dressed up for the graduation exercises of Cedar Grove

Elementary School. The stethoscope around his neck, his horn-rimmed glasses, and his deep bass voice all seemed assumed like poor theatrical disguises that did not succeed in lending credibility to a role.

Billie Jean, as she leapt to her feet, stood at attention, and registered deference, appeared to be play-acting, too. "Here's Dr. Temple, Miss Dove," she said.

"Oh?" said Miss Dove, sounding unconvinced.

"I am Dr. Baker's house officer," the interne announced from somewhere low in his visceral cavity.

Not knowing what a house-officer was, Miss Dove reserved comment.

"I hope you're fairly comfortable," he said. "I believe you're complaining of pain in the low dorsal region and of extended numbness in the right leg?"

"I am comfortable, thank you," said Miss Dove. She added: "And I did *not* complain."

"We use the word in a medical sense," said Dr. Temple. "I'll do a physical now before I take your history."

"You?" said Miss Dove.

"A superficial one," he assured her. "The fine points I'll leave for Dr. Baker."

Miss Dove sought words for protest. It had been strange enough to take orders from Thomas Baker and to be washed by Billie Jean; to lie here at the mercy of an owlish child with a false voice was ridiculous.

But Billie Jean had unbuttoned Miss Dove's bed-shirt. The doctor's stethoscope was cupped against her chest. Submission was the better part of dignity.

Lights were flashed in her eyes, up her nose, and down her throat. Her blood pressure was tested. She was prodded in the ribs, in the solar plexus, and in the abdomen.

"The belly muscles are remarkably firm," the young man said. His tone was so admiring that Miss Dove forgave him his indelicacy of diction. Coarseness, like an occupational disease, seemed to derive from the practice of medicine, and should—she supposed—be deplored rather than condemned. Even young Dr. Hurley said "belly."

When the examination was over Billie Jean retired from the room.

"Now we'll take your history," said Dr. Temple.

The questions he asked were personal, Miss Dove thought, to the point of irrelevance. However, she answered them.

She had been born in 1896. Her mother had been nineteen and her father thirty-eight. So far as she knew there had been no untoward circumstances attending her birth. "Naturally, my mother did not describe her confinement," she said.

Yes, she had siblings. Two sisters much younger than she. They lived three states away now, with growing families of their own. No. She had never been jealous of them.

(Jealous of Flora and Lucy! Those timorous creatures who echoed their husbands' opinions and jumped on chairs when they saw mice!

She had had the usual juvenile diseases.

(She was five when she had measles. She lay in the big, canopied four-poster in the company room with all her dolls to keep her company. Her mother sat by the window and sewed little doll dresses and told her fairy tales. Every evening her father brought her a new present. He brought her a music box that played Sur le Pont d'Avignon, a silver ring enameled with forget-me-nots, a string of coral beads, and a canary in a cage. He brought her a globe of the Earth.

He set the globe on a table and showed her the different seas and rivers and continents and countries. "This is France," he said. "Artists live there and the people speak differently from us. They say 'ma petite fille' for 'my little girl.' This is Switzerland where the mountains are covered with snow all year long. The mountains are called the Alps. And beyond the Alps lies Italy. See—it is shaped like a boot."

"Where is *here*?" she asked.

"Here is here," he said, showing her. "Here is home. But someday, when you're bigger, you and I will make the grand tour. We'll make a grander tour than anybody. We'll get on a boat and go down the Atlantic Ocean—" he traced the course with a finger "—and around the Horn, and up the Pacific. We'll visit China and eat bird's-nest soup. We'll go to India and see the fakirs—magic men—throw ropes into the air and climb up them."

"Can I climb?" she asked.

"No," he said. "If you did I'd be lonesome on the ground. We'll ride camels across the desert. We'll go to Venice where the streets are made of water and people go shopping in boats—gondolas they're called—instead of carriages."

The place-names filled her with enchantment. But what opened a real vista in her mind was the fact that the world was round. She had thought it was flat and four-cornered like the top of a candy box. If you walked far enough you would come to the edge and be in danger of falling off. She drifted into slumber on a new, slowly spinning sense of wonder.)

No, she told Dr. Temple, she did not suffer from headaches. She had no allergies. She was not often afflicted with respiratory infections. Her family tree revealed no epilepsy, night-blindness, eczema, or melancholy.

"What about your emotional life?" he asked.

"I beg your pardon?" said Miss Dove.

The doctor blushed which made him appear more

immature than ever. "Well—love, you know. And feelings of frustration. Inadequacy."

"I have never felt inadequate."

"The question was routine," he assured her. "Suppose we call your emotional life satisfactory?"

"That will be correct," said Miss Dove.

"Are you subject to fantasy?"

For a moment Miss Dove was not sure. Should she mention the floating sensation in the hospital corridor? Or the phantom children she had almost seen more than once in the empty geography room?

"Within reason," she said at last.

Dr. Temple did not press the matter.

"Thank you, Miss Dove," he said. "Dr. Baker will be in later, of course. And if there's anything I can do—" He smiled in an engaging, unprofessional way. "You and I are really old friends," he said. "In a manner of speaking, I've known you all my life."

"You have known *me*?" Miss Dove said. She scanned his face. It was vaguely familiar, but only vaguely.

"I'm Adams Temple," he told her. "My mother was a Liberty Hill girl."

"Angela Adams, of course," said Miss Dove. He had the same brown eyes, myopic and speculative, and the same conformation of the forehead—bulging over each eyebrow as if small, stubby horns were about to sprout through the bone. He had the same *enfant terrible* expression. "I should have known."

"Well, it's been a long time. Mother's family moved to Kansas when she was fourteen. But she remembers you."

"I remember her," Miss Dove said without marked enthusiasm. "She had an enquiring mind."

Angela Adams—who had received in the Judgment Book a C for Contentious—had taught Miss Dove, indirectly, valuable lessons in the technique of classroom management. Her name being what it was, she had sat on the front seat of the first row and had shown a tendency to lean forward with her elbow on her desk and her chin cupped in her palm instead of sitting erect with her hands folded. In the show-offy way in which most children enjoy turning cartwheels or somersaults, Angela had enjoyed mental gymnastics. "Why" and "how" were her favorite words— tiresome words to a very young instructress who was striving for a reputation for infallibility—and when Angela uttered them she was apt to look smug as if she thought: "*This* time I'll trip the teacher!"

Once, had she had the humility to leave well enough alone, she might have done just that.

Miss Dove had been reading aloud from a book on

the dietary habits of undomesticated animals. "Bears like honey," she read. "They are also fond of red ants which have a flavor similar to that of pickles."

Angela had waved her hand. "How does he know, Miss Dove?" she had demanded. "How does the author know what ants taste like?"

The thirty-nine other children in the room had fixed their trusting eyes upon Miss Dove, waiting for her answer. Then Angela, herself, saved the day. Brash with the imminence of victory, she had pushed her advantage too far.

"Did he eat an ant to see?" she had asked sarcastically. "Or did a bear tell him?"

The class had giggled. Ordinarily, Miss Dove frowned upon laughter, but this time it fell like music on her ear. She directed upon Angela her steady, solemn, scrutinizing gaze.

The child blushed. She folded her hands.

"Never *pretend* to be silly, Angela," Miss Dove said at last. She waited until a hush settled upon the room. Then she continued to read from the book: "The giraffe is a vegetarian. His long neck enables him to nibble the leaves of trees."

"She used to tell us stories about you," Dr. Temple said in the happy, nostalgic manner of a boy who is fond of his mother. "She said you reminded her of Mary Poppins."

"Mary Who?"

"Poppins. A magic English nanny in a fairy story. As soon as she walked into a nursery all babies stopped yelling and all buttons flew into the right buttonholes. According to Mother you had that effect, morally speaking, on a roomful of boisterous brats."

"It was not magic," said Miss Dove.

"Maybe character is a kind of magic," he said. "Mother said, too, that my Latin teacher in high school was like you. She kept us on our toes. Right now I could conjugate any verb, regular or irregular, you cared to give me."

Miss Dove did not care to give him a verb. "I am honored by the comparison," she said.

"Of course, she was more narrow-minded than you," he went on.

(And by what rule, pray, have you measured the breadth of my mind? Miss Dove asked silently.)

"It came from a surfeit of dead grammar, I guess. Do you know what she said to me when I left for college?"

"No," said Miss Dove.

Dr. Temple grinned reminiscently. "She said: 'Good-by, Adams. Don't get any new ideas!' "

Miss Dove saw nothing funny in the Latin teacher's

116

advice. She thought it shrewd and cogent and particularly sound for the son of Angela. "And did you?" she asked.

Dr. Temple laughed. "Very few," he admitted. "You know, there *aren't* many!"

With a nod he was gone. And it dawned upon Miss Dove that for all his volubility he had told her nothing of her physical condition. She said as much to her nurse.

"He's not in charge," said Billie Jean. "You're Dr. Baker's private patient."

"Then what is it—" Miss Dove began and her mouth went dry, "—what is it Dr. Baker suspects?"

Billie Jean shook her head. "He will tell you what you need to know."

"I see no occasion for mystery," said Miss Dove.

"Don't try to see," said Billie Jean. "Let *us* do the thinking!"

Let us do the thinking! Us! Billie Jean McVay whose expression when she'd looked at a little boy had been that of a gourmand surveying the cherry on top of a butterscotch sundae; Thomas Baker, the erstwhile clown, wit, wag, and ear-wiggler; and the complacent rosebud son of Angela Adams! Oh, no. *Miss Dove* did the thinking. It was the habit of a lifetime—the teacher's burden accepted long ago and never sloughed off for an instant! The modern fad of urging the young to "reason things out" she considered pedagogical laziness. Moreover, it encouraged agnosticism.

117

In the geography room *she* drew the conclusions. She doled them out to her pupils who received them whole, without analysis, and wrote them down between even margins in their notebooks.

But this was not the geography room.

Billie Jean knitted the toe of an enormous Argyle sock. Now and then, as if to tease her patient's mind away from the exploration of unprofitable channels, she quoted some artless pearl that had dropped from the milky lips of her little Ava.

Mrs. Lester Knight, Senior, stuck her head in at the door to report the condition of Lester, Junior. (Maternal fatuity had persuaded her that Miss Dove would be aching for such news.) "Tommy got his appendix just in time," she declared. "They were sizzling!"

Mr. Spivey came with his messages from the school. He delivered them in a bluff, hearty voice, resonant with spurious optimism.

Alexander Burnham came with the things he'd promised to bring. He stayed only a few minutes, confining his conversation to small, safe topics far removed from illness. A pair of robins were nesting in the ivy over the church door. Geoffrey Lyons, en route from New York to Hollywood, was stopping overnight with his brother. Jincey Baker was preserving her status quo and becoming rather impatient.

"He's a wonderful man," Billie Jean said when the minister had gone. "He believes in giving folks a second chance."

118

"Yes," said Miss Dove, "he is an ornament to his cloth."

But she was not concerned with Alexander's virtues. She was waiting for Thomas Baker.

Thomas did not appear until after supper. By that time, Billie Jean had been relieved by the night nurse, a dour, middle-aged woman who was not a native of Liberty Hill. She had been trained (as she made known immediately) to be a ward supervisor. At present she was resting between positions and had taken Miss Dove's case as a favor to the superintendent of the hospital.

"I am interested in the *theory* of nursing," she said.

"I see," said Miss Dove without pretending to be impressed. The mental keenness of the new nurse was probably greater than that of Billie Jean, she reflected, but her manual skill was less and she lacked humility. Routine duties of the bedside—the smoothing of pillows, the fetching of pans, and the counting of pulses —she regarded as unworthy of her talents, much as Mona Leckford regarded the teaching of Longfellow's poems to the fifth grade.

Thomas breezed into the room. He was dressed all in green. Green trousers and short sleeved blouse and a green, turban-like cap on his head. Miss Dove was startled. Had he, she wondered, been acting in a pageant to celebrate the arrival of Spring?

"This is the latest fashion for operating-room wear," said Thomas. "It's easy on the eyes. Did you think

I'd forgotten you?"

"No," said Miss Dove. She never fancied herself forgotten.

"I've been busy since I left you," Thomas said. "Dull, run-of-the-mine stuff that consumes time. First the Knight boy, of course—"

"Lester eats imprudently and too much," said Miss Dove. "Mrs. Knight informed me that his affected part was in danger of rupture."

Thomas laughed. "It was inflamed but not dramatic," he said. "Of course I told Jane it was sizzling. Give her something to brag about at the bridge table."

"I trust Lester's convalescence will be unimpeded," said Miss Dove.

"He's hungry already," said Thomas. "We'll have him up tomorrow." He gave Miss Dove's hand a perfunctory pat. "I just dropped by to see that you were being well treated."

But Miss Dove did not intend to let him escape so easily.

"I should like to ask a few questions concerning my own state of health," she said.

"Why, certainly," Thomas said, assuming the transparent disguise of candor that Miss Dove had come to recognize. "But I'm not sure I can answer them. Dr. Temple—did you know, by the way, that he's Angela Adams' son?"

"Yes," Miss Dove said indifferently, rejecting that decoy.

Dr. Temple's findings had all been negative, Thomas told her, which was good. Her blood pressure —systolic and dystolic—was ideal. Refraction of the eyes normal. Heart function unimpaired. No palpable abdominal masses.

"What is your guess?" asked Miss Dove.

"I don't guess," said Thomas. "Tomorrow we will do exhaustive tests. By Friday I should be able to speak with some degree of conviction. Until then—" He moved away. At the door he paused and turned to her. "Until then," he said, and his tone, though casual, carried an undertone of command, "I shall expect you, Miss Dove, to assume the virtue of docility."

"Yes, doctor," said Miss Dove. She closed her eyes and surrendered to the inevitable. Nothing had ever taxed her powers as did that passive act of resignation.

The weather changed in the night. Next day— Thursday—was raw and wet. At Cedar Grove School the children were restless. Mr. Spivey called a special assembly.

"As we're all sorry to know," he said, standing on the podium, "Miss Dove is in the hospital. But we're going right on with our geography work. We're not planning to let her down. I will take her place!"

A gust of giggles swept the air in the auditorium. The vision of Mr. Spivey with his bald, glittering head, his big Adam's apple, and his toothy grin sitting at Miss Dove's desk struck the student body as irresistibly comical.

"In other words," the principal shouted above the laughter, "we're all members of one team! Our quarterback has been injured in scrimmage, and I'm going to sub for her. I want to call the same plays she would call. But I don't know those plays as well as you do. So whenever I'm offside I want you to tell me. Okay?"

"Okay!" the audience responded.

"And we're all in there pitching together?"

"Sure!" Several boys spat on their hands and delivered imaginary round-house curves.

Later, incongruously throned in the geography room, he found the children as good as their promise.

At eight-forty-five the first grade filed in. Mr. Spivey, though a bachelor, was a family man at heart and like many such men—especially those who are amply built—he was charmed by littleness. The first-graders were his pets. He liked to give them lolly-pops, to join in their round games at recess, and to feel that they loved him. Generally, when they greeted him, their faces broke into merry smiles. Today, they kept their distance and forced him to keep his.

The first to enter the room was a lisping, pinafored girl known to all and sundry as Sister Abernathy. She blushed when she addressed the principal, but her face remained expressionless. "Good morning, Mithter Thpivey," she said.

"Good morning, Sister."

Sister shook her head. "Mith Dove callth me Annabel," she said. "And firtht you have to make me do my mannerth again becauthe I lithped."

Mr. Spivey cleared his throat. "Pronounce my name correctly," he said in a gruff voice. He felt like an ass. He twinkled at Sister.

She did not return his twinkle. "Good morning, Mi-sss-ter S-spivey," she said.

With the remainder of the class—excusing a couple of slips when he called Raymond "Buddy" and Susan "Peaches,"—he did moderately well.

Buddy—or Raymond—raised his hand. "Congratulations," he said.

"Thank you," said Mr. Spivey.

"You're welcome," said Raymond. He folded his hands upon his desk.

The others did likewise. They all sat there, perfectly silent, with their hands—as Mr. Spivey told Miss Ellwood later—closed together like the wings of sitting ducks, and their wide eyes fixed on him.

"What do I do now, Raymond?" he said at last.

"You say 'Attention, please. The lesson will begin,' " said Raymond.

Step by step, grade by grade, Mr. Spivey was helped through the day.

Acting on the principle that requires a captain to be the last man to leave a ship, Mr. Spivey made it his rule to remain in the building for a full hour after school was dismissed. Today, he was surprised that the music teacher, Miss Ellwood, had stayed too. He met her in the hall. She wore a red rain-cape of transparent plastic. Its hood cast a glow upon her complexion. Attached to the zippers on her rubber boots were tiny silver bells that tinkled when she walked.

"Some third grade moppets were making a dish-garden for Miss Dove," she explained. "I stayed to help them. You know what store she sets on neatness."

"That was awfully nice of you," said Mr. Spivey.

"She taught *me*," said Lorraine. Her blue eyes were misty. "Back in the dark ages."

Mr. Spivey understood that her reference to the far past of her childhood was intended to elicit from him a gallant contradiction. But *a deux* with a woman he was a bashful man.

"I took her classes and I feel I've been through a wringer," he said.

"I'll bet you do!" cried Lorraine. She laughed. A single tear shook out of one eye and was impaled, like a dewdrop, on the end of a lash.

"Such regimentation I've never seen," he declared. "And the queer thing is—the kids like it!"

"Yes. Deep down they do," said Lorraine. With a

dainty handkerchief that smelled of lily-of-the-valley she dabbed her eye. "She was a fabulous teacher! I mean she *is!*"

The spectacle of this gentle creature—all tenderness and femininity—weeping for an old tartar was infinitely touching to Mr. Spivey. "You're right to say '*is,*'" he said. "We must be positive and optimistic. I know Tom Baker is gravely concerned but—'no game is ever over 'til the final whistle blows!'"

"Life can be so sad," said Lorraine. "There she was reviewing the fourth grade for the proficiency tests! And with no warning—"

"I still don't approve of her didactic methods," said Mr. Spivey. "I believe in being pals with children. In classroom democracy."

"Oh, so do I!" said Lorraine.

"I don't approve of them," he went on musingly, "but I'll have to admit, they *work!* I figure it this way: Miss Dove is sincere. And kids are fair. You can't fool 'em. When they see somebody doing a sincere job, they know it. And they play ball!"

"It's so *big* of you to understand that," said Lorraine.

"I strive for tolerance," said Mr. Spivey. Then he suggested that Miss Ellwood let him drive her home. On the way they might stop at the Grill and Fountain for a cup of coffee. He would like to discuss with her a paper he was writing on the problems of extra-curricular activities in the elementary school.

"Oh, Mr. Spivey, that would be super!" cried Lorraine.

Thomas Baker once again brought Jincey her breakfast. He tried to maintain his usual bantering manner but his humor was forced and distrait.

"Are you worried about me or Miss Dove?" asked Jincey.

"Both," said Thomas. "But I have to stop worrying about you." He took her hand in his. "I have to shut you right out of my mind."

"Can you?"

"Yes." He gave her a level look. "I am Miss Dove's doctor."

Jincey wanted to cry. She was not in the least alarmed about herself. She was, in fact, one of those fortunate women in whom pregnancy induces a euphoric illusion of immunity to mischance. But she had counted on having her husband with her during labor much as she might have counted on having him at a dinner party.

"Well," she said, "I have a doctor too. Sam Tillet will probably be relieved not to have you messing 'round."

"I'll speak to Sam," said Thomas.

"I'll speak to him, myself," said Jincey. "In my interesting condition I'm still capable of using a telephone! Look, Tommy. Seriously, this is what I'll do. I'll move over to your mother's house today. Then you

126

won't need to give me a thought. Tomorrow, if I'm still navigating, I'll enter the hospital for the duration."

"That's a very smart idea," Thomas said, beaming upon his wife. She was ten years younger than he. He had married her for love—light-hearted love evoked by such charm as her coloring, the music in her laughter, and the exquisite balance of her flesh and bone—so that her gift for rationality, which he'd discovered after marriage, he thought of as a bonus he'd had no right to expect.

"I never was as stupid as I looked," said Jincey. She tossed her head. Loose tendrils of her tumbled hair glittered like delicate copper wires in the lamplight.

"Your hair's a halo," said Thomas.

"Miss Dove never thought so. She considered it Satan's own device to make me vain and divert little boys from their lessons!" Jincey laughed. "And she was so right! Once, I remember—" The gaiety went out of her voice and left it low and gentle and full of wood-pigeon notes; she crossed her arms as if to warm her recollection against her breast—"she took it in her hand and pulled it back and tied it with a little old piece of grocery string!"

Thomas had seen the teacher deal just so with other little girls. He stood in the doorway of the bedroom trying to visualize how Jincey must have looked—mortified or indignant?—for his wife's childhood, now that she was about to lose it finally and forever in the childhood of another, had begun to beguile his imagi-

127

nation. But Jincey's memory was not his to share because, though he had been, in a way, its hero, he had been so in absentia. And, really, it was not Jincey's either. It was more Miss Dove's.

The episode Jincey recalled had occurred in the geography room during World War Two. Miss Dove had been waiting for the sixth grade to file in when suddenly she had had the feeling of not being alone. Someone or something was moving about the room. Over there, near the sand table, it paused and looked at her. But even when the presence glided along the wall behind her; even when she heard—or almost heard—a new stick of chalk squeaking on the blackboard, Miss Dove did not turn around. She knew, of course, that nobody was there. Her nerves were playing tricks on her again. Miss Dove did not believe in nerves.

Through the open door she watched the sixth graders come out of the music room down the hall. They came out with a rush, as if for two minutes of freedom between classroom and classroom they were borne along upon some mass exhilaration. They always left the music room in that fashion but today they managed to be noisier than usual. It was the season, she supposed. The day was warm and the children were restless as the weather. There was a sharp sound as of someone being spanked with a book; there was a voice saying, "Double dare, Randy!"; there was a breathless giggling.

But as they approached Miss Dove's room they pulled their excitement in like proud but well-broken ponies. They greeted her politely and went to their places. At a nod from her they took their seats.

Jincey Webb, Miss Dove noticed without enthusiasm, had a permanent wave. Yesterday her carrot-colored mane had been neatly braided and pulled back from her serious freckled face. Now it hung to her shoulders, a bushy mop of undulations and frizz. It hung on her mind, too; that was plain to see. Jincey's expression was one of utter and enviable complacency. It seemed doubtful that a long lifetime of repeated triumphs could again offer her an achievement so sublime with self-satisfaction.

Randy Baker wiggled his ears at Jincey. Miss Dove looked at him. His eyes grew round with innocence. His ears grew very still.

Miss Dove kept looking at him, but she had stopped seeing him. Instead, she was seeing his brother Thomas, who had sat there at Randy's desk years before, with the same film of specious virtue over the mischief in his eyes. And then she saw Thomas on a raft in the Pacific. She did not see him as they had described him in the papers—skin and bones and haggard young face overgrown with a rough, wild beard. The Thomas she saw looked like Randy. He had braces on his teeth and a dimple in his chin. And he was all alone in the dismal gray mountains of the sea.

A wave of giddiness swept over her, but she did not

sit down. It was nothing. It had happened to her off and on all year, and it had always passed.

"Open your notebooks, class," she said.

It was Tuesday and Tuesday was note-book day in the geography room. Miss Dove had so ordained it when she had first assumed control there and she had never toyed with the notion of changing Tuesday's function. She was not a woman to toy with notions. On that day each week her pupils inscribed on ruled pages such verbal matter as their teacher believed suitable to their stage of development. The first grade, for example, might write—copying from the board—, "The yak is a very useful animal" and, later, the more complicated sentence about the camel. The third grade made lists of the states in a prescribed order, they began with Maine and went down the Atlantic coastline to Florida and then, moving over to Alabama, up to Michigan, and so on. The sixth graders, who were being prepared by degrees for the inescapable perils of independent thinking that would beset them soon, copied a statement of fact that contained an aphorism and enlarged upon it in their own words. Miss Dove had a goodly store of these geographical maxims. "The trade winds maintain a steady course" she would often write, or "Above the fiftieth parallel life requires hardihood," or "Gibraltar is proof against the erosion of the waters." She was about to choose from one of these when a boy on the back row choked on a clandestine peppermint, sputtered, bulged his eyes, turned purple in the face and was obliged to leave the room for water.

Miss Dove watched him go, but her mind watched two small boys who had long since departed from Cedar Grove.

She had come on those lads at the drinking fountain. (They'd had no business at the fountain; it was

their library period. But the librarian was lax.) They had been discussing her.

"I bet Miss Dove could lick Joe Louis," one of them had said.

"Who? That old stick?" the other one had jeered. "I could beat her with my little finger!"

He had glanced up to see Miss Dove looking down at him. She had looked at him for a long time. Her gray eyes were expressionless. The tip of her long nose was pink, but no pinker than normal. At last she had spoken.

"Thomas Baker," she had said in the tone of one making a pure observation, "you talk too much, don't you?"

"Yes, ma'am," Thomas had said in a tiny voice. He had gone off without getting any water. For a long time afterwards he sweated when he thought of the incident. He could not know that Miss Dove remembered too. But she did.

Ever since Pearl Harbor Miss Dove had been troubled. She lived quite alone, for her sisters were married by then and her mother was dead, and one evening while she was correcting papers she sensed, with that uncanny extra-perception of the teacher, that something had intruded upon her solitude. She looked quickly about her sitting-room. A curtain rustled in a puff of breeze; her grandmother's whatnot cast a grotesque shadow on the polished floor; a finger of lamplight picked out a gold title on one of her father's old brown travel books. There was nothing else. But the red correction pencil shook in her fingers; for a moment her throat constricted in a spasm of desolate, unaccountable grief and a conviction of her own unworthiness. Miss Dove had never before felt unworthy in all her life.

After that the thing happened frequently, until at last she saw who the intruders were. They were the children she had taught long ago.

War had scattered those children. There was a girl —a vain, silly little piece she had been—who was a nurse on Corregidor. At least, when last heard of she had been on Corregidor. One of the boys was dead in Tunisia. Others were on the Anzio beachhead, or in the jungles of New Guinea, or in the flak-brightened sky over Germany. But they came back to Miss Dove. She saw them as they had been at seven, at ten, at twelve. Only they had a beauty she had not seen in them then. They lifted their faces like starry morning flowers. Their limbs quivered with the unreasoned joy of childhood. And then, as Miss Dove looked at them, they grew still. Their faces paled. They clasped their little hands. They faded and were gone.

The child who came oftenest was Thomas Baker. The town paper had been full of Thomas. His ship had been bombed, his officers killed, and Thomas had taken over. A hundred men owed their lives to his presence of mind. For days he had floated on a raft with no food and only the water in his canteen. When they picked him up his tongue had protruded from his mouth, black and swollen with thirst. That was what got Miss Dove—he had run out of water.

The Thomas who came to stand before her now was a sturdy boy in knickers. He held his chin at a cocky angle, but the dimple in it trembled. He ran the tip of his tongue over his lips.

But the children came only at night. When day-

133

light returned Miss Dove could believe she had been the victim of waking dreams. She would eat her customary boiled egg and her whole-wheat toast; she would take a vitamin pill with her orange-juice; she would walk forth at her usual pace and assume her usual role of unshakable authority. The children at the school would seem to have little in common with those graceful and evanescent figures that haunted her. And no intruders dared invade the geography room. Or they hadn't until today.

The boy who had choked returned. Another boy, in the row by the window, cleared his throat. One in the middle row followed suit. Soon the whole room was dotted with the sound, a rough "h-hrmph" like frogs in a marsh. Miss Dove knew what the sound meant. It was the school's traditional signal—a kind of dare. She had heard other teachers speak of it in exasperation. It was the first time it had occurred in her room.

Slowly Randy Baker raised his hand. The sounds stopped. Silence like a caught breath hung on the room. Miss Dove could see beads of sweat on Randy's brow. His open palm was damp and gleaming.

"Yes, Randolph?" she said.

Randy stood up. Miss Dove's pupils always stood when they addressed her. He smoothed his plump stomach with his hand. "I got a letter from Tommy yestiddy," he said.

"*Received*, Randolph," said Miss Dove. "You received a letter from your brother *yesterday*. That was nice."

"Yes, Miss Dove," said Randy. He hesitated. Clearly, he was floundering. "He sent me a dollar he won playing poker in the convalescent hospital."

"I am sorry to hear that Thomas gambles," said Miss Dove, "but we are all very proud of his war record. If you have nothing more interesting to tell us you may take your seat, Randolph."

"H-hr-rmph!" went the boy behind Randy.

"He's been decorated," said Randy, "for bravery beyond the call of duty." The high words seemed to inspirit him. "He sent a message to the class."

"Did you bring the letter?" asked Miss Dove. "If so, you may read that part aloud."

Randy took an air-mail envelope from his hip pocket.

The class stirred. The ghost of a titter rippled the air.

"Attention, please," said Miss Dove.

Randy opened the letter. The paper was smudged and crumpled. Obviously, it had suffered many readings in many hands. Randy cleared his throat. The sound he made was not a link in the chain signal. Miss Dove could tell the difference. "It's sort of long," Randy demurred hopefully.

"We can spare the time," she said.

Randy began to read. His voice was high and clear; it had the girlish sweetness that comes just before the breaking point.

"The funny thing about the world," Randy read, "is that it looks just like you think it does. When they flew me back to Cal. in a hospital plane I looked down and, heck, kid, I might as well have been looking at those diagrams on the geography board back in dear (ha, ha!) ole Cedar Grove. I spotted a peninsula. A body of water almost entirely surrounded by land. I saw some atolls too. And they really are made in rings like doughnuts with palm trees sprouting out of the cake part and blue water in the hole in the middle. The water is the color of that blue chalk I swiped once and drew a picture of Miss Dove on the sidewalk with. Remember?"

He swallowed hard.

"Proceed, Randolph," said Miss Dove.

"You want to know if I was scared when the little yellow insects from—" Randy blushed but went on— "from hell"—in his embarrassment he brought out the word with unnecessary force—"dive-bombed us. The answer is, you bet. But it came to me in a flash that I wasn't much scareder than I was that time ole lady Dove caught me bragging about how I could beat her up at the drinking fountain. 'I didn't run that time,' I told myself, 'so I won't run now.' Besides there wasn't much place to run to."

The class laughed nervously.

"And later," Randy read on doggedly, "when I was bobbing up and down like Crusoe on my raft, what do you guess I thought about? It wasn't any pin-up girl. It was Miss Dove. I thought about the fishy stare she used to give us when we needed a drink of water. So to make my supply hold out I played I was back in the geography room. And even after the water was gone I kept playing. I'd think, 'The bell is bound to ring in a few minutes. You can last a little longer.' It took the same kinds of guts in the Pacific it did in school. Tell that to the guys in Cedar Grove." Randy stopped abruptly.

"Hr-hrmph!" went someone.

"Is that the end?" asked Miss Dove.

Randy looked directly at her. For a fleeting moment she thought he was going to say yes. If he did, that would be that.

Randy shook his head. "No, Miss Dove," he said. "There's a little more." His face turned the color of a ripe tomato. "He says here"—Randy gulped—"he says"—Randy took a deep breath—"he says: 'Give the terrible Miss Dove a kiss for me!' "

Miss Dove came down from her platform. She inclined her head with her cheek turned in Randy's direction.

"Well, Randolph," said Miss Dove, "I am waiting."

There was an electric stillness that was followed, as the full meaning of her words penetrated the children's consciousness, by a gasp. Randy folded the letter and put it back into his pocket. Then he began to walk toward the teacher. He walked with the deliberate stoicism of a martyr going to the chopping block. He did not come any closer than he had to. He leaned forward stiffly from the waist and placed his puckered lips against her cheek. His kiss resounded, a small explosion in the room.

"Thank you, Randolph," said Miss Dove. "You may give Thomas my regards." She straightened up and faced the class. To her surprise, nobody was grinning.

Jincey Webb spoke. She did not raise her hand for permission. She just spoke out.

"It's like a medal," Jincey said softly. "It's like he pinned a medal on Miss Dove."

For a moment a lamp seemed to burn behind her face. Then over the light swept a shadow. It was as if Jincey had glimpsed some universal beauty—of sorrow, perhaps, or of nobility—too poignant for her youth to bear. She began to cry. She flopped her head down on her desk with her red hair falling forward and spreading out like a crinkly fan.

All the other girls wept with her. All the boys stared sternly into space.

For the first time in her teaching career Miss Dove was at a loss. She wanted to make a speech. She wanted to say something beautiful and grateful about what life really meant to her, about the overwhelming generosity of children. But the words would not come.

Then she saw that what she had to thank her class for was not generosity at all. It was something much better than that and much harder to come by. It was justice.

And as she realized that, she realized also that she was neglecting her duty. The first duty of a teacher was to preserve order.

She fished a piece of string out of a receptacle on her desk. She walked down the aisle to Jincey Webb. She took Jincey's hair, that marvel of art and nature, and bunched it in her hand. She tied it securely at the nape of Jincey's neck with the little bit of grocery string.

"Now it will be out of your way," she said.

At the sound of her voice, cool, precise, and usual, the children rallied. They sat erect. They blew their noses with clean handkerchiefs. They folded their hands on their desks.

"Pens in position, class," she said.

A transient mist stung her eyes. Through it, as through a prism, the children glowed. Freckles, cow-licks, pinafores, and polo shirts seemed bathed in a rainbow iridescence. Her love flowed out to those children—to those with their pen points poised above their paper and to those in the far places she had once helped them locate on the map. It did not flow tenderly like a coddling mother's love. It flowed on a fierce rush of hope and pride, the way an old general's heart might follow his men into battle.

She went to the blackboard and picked up a piece of chalk. "Above the fiftieth parallel—" wrote the terrible Miss Dove.

The Thursday Bridge Club was as select and small as a bridge club could be. It was composed of four young matrons who took it seriously. But today, at Mrs. Reese's house, the play was erratic.

"If you hadn't finessed the ten we'd have made our contract," Mrs. Reese said testily to her partner, Mrs. Knight. "The board was good."

"I can't keep my mind on the game," Mrs. Knight said. "I've been through too much. Lester, Junior's, narrow squeak and Miss Dove paralyzed!"

"Is that what it is? Paralysis?"

"She can't move her leg. A rose by any other name—"

"Tommy hasn't arrived at a diagnosis," said Mrs. Briggs who, as Jincey Baker's sister, presumed to a knowledgeable air.

"What does he think?"

"Tommy's a clam," Mrs. Briggs said just airily enough to convey the impression that she, alone, was in the surgeon's confidence. "But he's deeply concerned. He told Jince this morning that she'd have to manage having the baby with no help from him!"

"The poor child! If there's ever a time a woman needs her husband—" Mrs. Evans sighed sentimentally. Her own husband, John Wesley, had been conspicuously drunk throughout her hours of discomfort preceding Victoria's birth. But he had stayed at her bedside looking like a stricken deer, matching her groans with his, and protesting his devotion in flowery phrases as heart-felt as they were maudlin.

"Jince has plenty of spunk," Mrs. Briggs said. "She knows her duty as a doctor's wife."

"Besides, Sam Tillet is an excellent obstetrician," said Mrs. Reese.

"I saw her yesterday," Mrs. Knight said, trying to sound modest. "Miss Dove, I mean."

"You weren't supposed to," said Mrs. Briggs. "Tommy's discouraging visitors."

"I just wanted to reassure her about Lester, Junior. You know when they opened him up his appendix were sizzling."

But the club had heard all it cared to hear about Lester, Junior.

"Appendix *was*. Not *were*," said Mrs. Briggs. "How did she look?"

"Like herself," Mrs. Knight replied. "Only—well, different in a way I can't explain. Gentler. Like an old lion with its teeth pulled."

"Dear Lord!" Mrs. Reese said. "It breaks my heart to think of the terrible Miss Dove being *gentle!*"

"We saw her on her way to the hospital," said Mrs. Evans. "Tom and Sandy were carrying her. She was sitting on their hands just like it was nothing out of the way at all. Not batting an eye."

"Miss Dove has never batted an eye," Mrs. Knight declared on a note of almost familial pride.

"Wes knew something serious had happened. He acted like he'd seen a ghost," Mrs. Evans said. Not being a born Liberty Hillian, she thought her husband's reactions vastly more important than the teacher's illness. "He'd been under the weather, you know—"

Her companions nodded. They had all observed Mr. Evans' antics at a recent country club dance.

"—and he was about to take a morning pick-me-up. But he didn't. He swallowed an egg instead."

"Maybe that will prove the turning point of his life," said Mrs. Reese. Her sarcasm was lost upon Mrs. Evans.

"I have faith that it will," declared Mrs. Evans in whom faith died hard. "He said he was through forever." Her face was suffused with hope and happiness. "God moves in a mysterious way!"

This was too much for Mrs. Knight. "I don't believe for an instant that God was thinking of Wes Evans' habits," she said, "when He struck down Miss Dove!"

"Oh, no! I didn't mean that exactly!" Mrs. Evans cried. "I'm dreadfully sorry about Miss Dove. You must all have been devoted to her."

"If we were we didn't know it," said Mrs. Reese. "She turned us to stone."

"Remember the poem Geoff wrote?"

"Remember the clean handkerchiefs and the margins?"

"The laundry soap?"

"Remember in the first grade how she told us about the camel who was 'not a pretty beast' but who could go 'many days without water'?" said Mrs. Briggs. "And how she stared at us 'til we knew she meant we weren't to hang around the drinking fountain?"

"Can anybody bound Russia?" asked Mrs. Knight.

"No. Not now," said Mrs. Reese.

The three women were drawn backward in time. They returned to a safe charted world where colors were paint-box bright, boundaries stayed the same, and all the ideas they could conceivably use were handed down to them, complete with punctuation, from a raised dais.

"I was counting on her to break Snookie of chewing her hair the way she broke me," Mrs. Briggs said almost petulantly. Then she began to cry. So did Mrs.

Knight and Mrs. Reese.

They sat there at a bridge table in a pretty living room—three plumpish, prosperous women, with pearls on their ear lobes—and wept for their childhood. Mrs. Evans looked on in silent sympathy. After a moment, she managed to squeeze out a tear of her own.

Mrs. Briggs fumbled in the pocket of her purple gabardine suit. "Damn!" she said. "I haven't got a handkerchief!"

"Take mine," said Mrs. Evans.

"What would Miss Dove think of this?" Mrs. Briggs sniffled. "At my age—having to borrow a hanky!"

"And saying a great big D!" added Mrs. Knight.

Mrs. Reese rose abruptly. "We'll have to pull ourselves together, girls. Life must go on!" She went out to the kitchen to fetch hot coffee and patty shells filled with creamed chicken and—since the club was dieting —a dish of crystallized ginger in lieu of a heavy sweet.

The local Rotarians had convened for their weekly luncheon meeting. Alexander Burnham had said grace. The shrimp cocktails had been served. Suddenly Mr. Porter, who was a founder and president-emeritus of the club, and who saw no reason to

address the chair before he took the floor, struck his knife against his cocktail bowl. He struck so hard that a blob of red sauce leapt out, as if in fright, and landed upon the white tablecloth.

"Boys," said Mr. Porter, rising to his full height, which was imposing in spite of the stoop of age, "it is my considered opinion, after a lifetime's observation,

145

that a good business man's heart is not in his chest, but in his wallet."

This remark was greeted with polite laughter.

But Mr. Porter had not meant to be witty. He beetled his brows, craned his long, gaunt old neck and looked severely at his audience. He lifted his water goblet.

"Before I proceed," he said in a voice that creaked with emotion, "let me propose a toast. To the terrible Miss Dove!"

The Rotarians drank. They set their goblets down. They applauded. Then, on a common impulse, they squirmed in their chairs. They planted their feet firmly upon the carpet. They straightened their backs. A few of them folded their hands.

In the hospital, undergoing those tests that Thomas Baker had called exhaustive and that were, she discovered, certainly exhausting, Miss Dove did not imagine that her plight created any stir of feeling in Liberty Hill. She considered herself a private person, moving in a private orbit. That this orbit, this small, limited range of endeavor, should be multiplied into a series of rings—ever-widening as time went on, like those rings that originate from a pebble cast into a still pond, had never occurred to her.

She did not undervalue her talents. She knew she was a good teacher of elementary geography. She knew she had a gift for molding the clay of children's minds and laying upon them a hard protective glaze of discipline. But that was all in her job. If she did not forget her pupils after she was through with them, that was only because she was, by an accident of nature, a person of retentive memory. She remembered them without illusion—fancying that they hadn't altered much for better or worse; and so, she presumed, they remembered her. To believe that wholesome fear would some day be transmuted into affection would have struck her as nonsense. That was a pathetic fallacy embraced by mothers, not teachers!

And even if she had not scorned that sentimental dream she would hardly have indulged in it today. Today was here and now. In this hospital. With this pain. Miss Dove's joints were tapped with a small hammer. Her spine was pierced by a needle. In her bed she was rolled from strange place to strange place. Steel plates were clasped to her head and her brain waves recorded. All the bones in her body were X-rayed.

Thomas was in constant attendance. He promised to be with her through all her tests unless some emergency arose too complicated for the interne to handle.

"And Adams Temple is a good boy. He can handle most things," he said. "I'll be sorry to see him go."

"He is not staying?"

"No. He's only temporary. He finished med school at Christmas and starts a Hopkins interneship in July," Thomas told her. "He's helping us out in the meantime. I gather his mother wanted him to get acquainted with Liberty Hill."

"His mother had an enquiring mind," said Miss Dove.

Thomas laughed. "I know what you mean. Adams gets a bit above himself at times." He turned to Billie Jean. "And now, Mrs. Green, the percussion hammer please."

Thomas' attitude altered subtly. It became aloof in a way that gave Miss Dove confidence. His whole attention was directed upon his investigation. His eyes had a penetrating look. He was gentle. He was deft. But he did not apologize when he was obliged to hurt her. Only once—just after the first spinal puncture—did she see him wince with compassion.

(All the Bakers shrank from causing pain, Miss Dove remembered. It was a family trait. Through the haze of her own pain she seemed to see those boys again—Thomas, Charles, Randolph, and Sterling! They were all the same size. All about ten or twelve years old and as alike as four paper dolls cut from one folded sheet of paper. They all wore red sweaters—it was the same sweater, of course, passed down from first to last—and brown corduroy pants with leather patches on the knees. They all had candid eyes and

148

unexpected fits of shyness that came from sympathy.)

But as if he guessed her thoughts, Thomas gave her a strict, impersonal look. And as the day wore on she ceased to think of him as one of the Baker boys. She ceased to think of herself as a teacher. He was a doctor. She was a patient. Her will hung suspended in his.

With a sense of mingled triumph and distress, Thomas perceived all this. He had taken a high hand with Miss Dove because he had felt that no other hand would do. He had won the struggle for ascendancy. But his victory was not very sweet.

The results of the examinations were far from encouraging. Each test drew Thomas closer to the diagnosis he dreaded. But he remained methodical and open to persuasion. He reserved his conclusion. He had learned how to do that in laboratories and dissecting rooms. He had learned it in the Navy. He had learned it even earlier in the geography room at Cedar Grove School.

How he had fought against that lesson! How he had longed to be important enough to give orders to Miss Dove.

Once, he remembered, he had snitched a piece of blue chalk and had drawn her caricature on the cement walk that led to the school. It had been, in his opinion and that of his friends, a work of genius done in heroic proportions and embellished with time-honored details of humor. Miss Dove had been depicted as nine feet tall. She had been smoking a cigar and holding in one upraised hand a large bottle marked WHISKEY. Hidden in the shrubbery, Thomas had waited to see what the original would do when she saw the portrait.

At last she had come out of the building. She had seen the picture. She had given it a cool, appraising glance and had walked across it as if it did not exist.

And suddenly, watching her retreating back—the hat, the neck, the ball of hair, and the stick-like ankles beneath the dark skirt—the boy had been aghast. He had glimpsed a haughty loneliness that had struck him somehow—though he wouldn't have used that word—as being universal. For the first time in his life he had experienced empathy, the least comfortable of human emotions.

Heavy rain had fallen that night. Next morning only a faint blue stain remained on the pavement. But for some time thereafter Thomas had avoided the front walk to the school.

With all that in mind, he found the mild, obedient face of the woman on the bed almost more than he could bear.

But after the final X-rays, when he was helping Billie Jean guide the patient's bed back to her room, an incident occurred to show him that Miss Dove was still Miss Dove.

Lester Knight, Junior, having accomplished the rapid recovery of which callow youth is capable, was making full use of a wheel chair. He had escaped from the children's ward and was speeding along the corridors, careening around corners, and whooping with mirth at the alarm he occasioned to pedestrians.

Thomas started for him but jumped back when Lester, drunk with freedom, aimed the chair in his direction.

"Lester," Miss Dove said quietly. Her tone was level and calm and perfectly usual.

Lester braked his chair. His eyes bulged.

Miss Dove gave him a long gelid look. "You may return to your room," she said.

"Yes, Miss Dove," said Lester. His voice squeaked.

A pursuing nurse with cap askew and expression

irate, seized him, chair and all, and rolled him away.

"I hope she smacks his jaws," said Billie Jean.

"Ah, Miss Dove!" said Thomas. He bent over her. Had it not been for her eyes—the eyes that had quenched the spirits of Lester, Junior—he might have saluted her as his little brother had once done for him.

At the door of her room he left her.

"Tomorrow afternoon we'll talk," he said. "Until then I want you to put all this business out of your mind."

He hurried away.

"We won't worry about tomorrow, will we?" said Billie Jean. "Oh, my! Here we are in a greenhouse."

The room was banked with hothouse flowers. On the bureau, the table, and even in corners on the floor they bloomed.

"There are too many," said Miss Dove. "Restraint is the better part of beauty. I will keep the white azalea. Later I can set it outdoors in a sheltered place. Please dispose of the others."

"Yes, Miss Dove," said Billie Jean. She looked as disappointed as a child.

"There must be less fortunate patients who would enjoy them," said Miss Dove.

Billie Jean brightened. The prospect of walking through the wards playing Lady Bountiful to "the less fortunate" was to her taste. After she had completed the last of her errands she sat down and took out her fountain pen.

"I saved the cards," she said. "And I borrowed some stationery. If you'd like me to write the thank-you notes I'd be glad to."

"That would be obliging," said Miss Dove. The notion of using Billie Jean as a social secretary had novelty. The notion of keeping her quiet had charm.

"Will you dictate them?"

"No," said Miss Dove. "Use your discretion, Mrs. Green. Only avoid the fulsome."

The room was restful. The dwarf azalea tree was very pure in color and line against the blue wall. There was no sound except for the Spring rain murmuring against the window and for Billie Jean breathing hard (like a child taking a proficiency test) in the throes of literary composition.

"I've finished," Billie Jean said after a while. "I said the same thing to everybody." She handed a sheet of paper to Miss Dove. "Is it all right?"

Miss Dove perused the sample.

"Dear Mr. Porter," it read, "at the request of Miss Dove I am advising you that she is thrilled by your florial offering. The sympathy of friends brings sunshine to shut-ins. Cordially yours, Billie Jean Green, R.P.N."

Miss Dove, being totally unendowed with humor, had no inclination to laugh. Her inclination, arising from established editorial habit, was to pick the letter to pieces—to point out its errors in tone and spelling. But something in Billie-Jean's face—a look of vanity as

154

innocent as the flowers of Spring—deterred her.

"What does R.P.N. stand for?" she asked.

"Registered Practical Nurse," said Billie Jean. "How is the letter?"

"It is very—" Miss Dove sought a word that would carry truth without a wound—"very genteel."

The word was perfect. "Oh," said Billie Jean, "I'll tell Bill!"

"You may, Mrs. Green," Miss Dove said.

Billie Jean brought a damp cloth and washed her patient's face. She did it gently. She was a good nurse, Miss Dove reflected—more gifted in providing kindness and creature comfort than in verbal expression. She was a woman who had found her sphere.

"You know, Miss Dove," Billie Jean blurted out suddenly, "I'm not really Mrs. Green!"

Miss Dove said nothing.

"I took the name for little Ava's sake," said Billie Jean.

Miss Dove still remained silent.

"I was way out there in Detroit!" Billie Jean continued. Her tone was pleading.

"Virtue knows no geography," said Miss Dove.

"I was on the night-shift," said Billie Jean. "It got me all mixed up. I'd never been anywhere before. Mamma was always careful with me—she never let me go on high school hay rides or anywhere much except church socials. I wasn't very mature!"

"No," agreed Miss Dove.

"All the fellows wanted to take me out. I guess it went to my head. There was this one fellow—I didn't know he was married—that was wonderful to me. I—I gave him too much. In other words—"

"You need not elaborate," said Miss Dove.

"He was so good looking and big," said Billie Jean. "And I was so homesick. You know how it is!"

"I do *not* know how it is," said Miss Dove. "But I know that right is right and wrong is wrong."

"That's what Bill says. Those very words," said Billie Jean. "So little Ava came way out in Detroit." (She seemed to imply that the infant had been clever to manage being born in that outlandish place.) "I could have left her for adoption. There was an agency wanted her. And there was this old childless couple—the lady was over forty—that offered me three thousand dollars! But—well, she was mine. She was like home-folks. And how did I know other folks would raise her right?"

"A child is a responsibility," said Miss Dove.

"So I brought her home and told that tale about my husband being killed. Mamma said she'd keep Ava while I worked. I talked to Reverend Burnham and Dr. Hurley. They got me into the practical nursing course. So here I am!"

Miss Dove sighed. She was not astonished. She knew that in the great world, both in and out of literature, such things happened. Even in the smaller world of Liberty Hill they were, though scarcely com-

monplace, by no means unheard of. And after half a
biblical lifetime in a public school she was immunized
to astonishment.

Her sigh was for William Holloway.

"And why," she said, "did you confide in me,
Mrs.—?"

"Billie Jean," the nurse said. "It was because you
said that about the letter. I'm not as genteel as you
think and I couldn't deceive you."

"Deceit is a tangled web," said Miss Dove.

"I had to tell Bill too," Billie Jean said. "He's like
you. A person you tell the truth to."

"Ah!" said Miss Dove.

"He was cut up," Billie Jean said. "He was furious.
He didn't date me for a week. And then he said he'd
marry me anyhow but if he ever caught me doing anything unrespectable—even looking fresh at a fellow or
smoking in public—he'd"—she paused dramatically—
"he'd *take his belt to me!*"

Somehow Miss Dove felt sanguine as to William's
domestic future. He was one of those elect who had
the gift of authority and the nerve to use it. And
Billie Jean was born to love a master.

As she fed Miss Dove her evening meal (asparagus
soup and apricot whip) the nurse was silent. Her expression was subdued, but not uncheerful. She was
brooding, no doubt, upon Patrolman Holloway's
strong right arm. At last she said: "I guess I'm one
of those that have to learn the hard way."

"We all are, Billie Jean," said Miss Dove.

When the night nurse arrived she went about her duties more efficiently than before. She maintained her air of being above the station in which she found herself, but her hands were gentler. Miss Dove noticed the difference. She guessed its cause. The woman suspected now that her patient was more than ordinarily ailing. Miss Dove was no longer a negligible old school-teacher with a backache. She was an "interesting case" and, as such, cast dignity upon ministrations performed in her behalf.

A small quick flame of fear leapt in her mind. For an instant it burned steady, throwing its beams into the amorphous shadows of the future. But Miss Dove refused to look where the beams pointed.

Thomas Baker had directed her to put the whole business out of her mind. Once she had exacted obedience of him. Now that roles were reversed, she must allow him to exact it of her.

In the geography room each class, each day, was allotted a short reading period. For a prescribed number of minutes the children—keeping their posture correct and being careful not to move their lips or contort their features—had perused a prescribed number of pages. When the time was up they closed their books and listened while Miss Dove explained to them what they had just read. To read ahead—to go on, undirected, into the next chapter—was a graver misdemeanor than to fall behind. The latter was merely slothful; the former was impudent and dangerous. In such unguided sorties children were likely to collect odd impressions and form unsound opinions. The greenhorn mind, Miss Dove felt, should do its first traveling abroad in company and on a *guided* tour.

Thomas had told her, in effect, that she must not "read ahead." She forbade her fancy to turn the page.

She slept through the night and, if she dreamed at all, her dreams were of that childlike, inconsequential kind—scarcely more than echoes of a lullaby—that dissolve with returning consciousness. She awoke to hear Billie Jean telling the night nurse good-by and to see that the rain had stopped. Beyond her window the sky was opalescent gray—the color of April itself.

The morning passed quietly. Miss Dove had her bath and breakfast. Billie Jean turned the toe of the big sock. The interne made rounds.

Jincey Baker stopped in, wearing a ruffled negligee and looking remarkably like a little girl who was playing at pregnancy with a pillow stuffed under her waistband.

She had been admitted to the hospital, Jincey said, more for Tommy's peace of mind than anything. She was several days past term. If nothing definite had happened by Saturday night, Sam Tillet had promised to give Nature a nudge.

"Whatever Dr. Tillet suggests will be wise," Billie Jean said primly.

"Of course," said Jincey, making it plain that she did not question the wisdom of her obstetrician. "Right now he suggests that I keep walking. I peeped in to ask Miss Dove to wish me luck."

"I do, Virginia," said Miss Dove.

When Jincey had left to continue her promenade Billie Jean said: "I used to think she was the snootiest, dumbest brat in Liberty Hill. But she's really a good kid. She hasn't hardly seen her husband for days, and not a cheep out of her!"

"A physician cannot call his time his own," said Miss Dove.

"Nor an officer of the law, either," Billie-Jean added smugly. "It's like the old folks say. 'Men must work and women must weep.'"

"I consider that an effete philosophy," said Miss Dove.

"Oh, so do I!" agreed Billie-Jean, who had no inkling of the meaning of effete.

More blossoms arrived. There were two mixed bouquets from the florist (Miss Dove dispensed with them) and the dish garden that the pupils of the third grade had made under Miss Ellwood's supervision. The dish was a biscuit pan filled with moss and bordered with ferns and hepatica. In the moss was stuck a seedling cedar and nearby, in the exact center of the pan, sat a rectangular building made of red cardboard upon which the pattern of bricks had been marked in white ink.

"It's Cedar Grove!" said Billie Jean. "Oh, isn't it sweet!"

"Yes," said Miss Dove. As she examined the arrangement of the garden she saw something sweeter still. She saw a group of children absorbed in a task and aiming at perfection. She was aware of a constriction in her throat. "The ink-work is laudably neat," she said. "You may place it on the windowsill."

Just before noon there was a message from the hospital receptionist. Two out-of-town visitors wished to see Miss Dove. One had telephoned to ask permission. The other was waiting in the lobby.

"Who are they?" Miss Dove asked Billie-Jean.

"Well, they're not birds of a feather, as the old folks say," said Billie Jean. "One is Mr. Lyons, the writer from New York. The other is Fred Makepeace." She looked haughty. "I suppose you know where he resides!"

"I do know," said Miss Dove. Fred was an inmate of a prison camp. "I shall be glad to see them both. They are my former pupils."

"*Mr.* Makepeace," said Billie-Jean, with a flounce of her head, "was sure of his welcome. *He's* already come. If you don't mind, I'll wait outside." She walked stiffly away. Obviously, as the fiancee of a policeman, she intended to preserve herself from association with felons.

Fred Makepeace entered the room. He was a lean,

161

sandy-haired man in the middle thirties. He was dressed in blue serge. A snow-white handkerchief protruded from his breast pocket. His shoes were polished to a lustre. He walked on the balls of his feet and his manner, as he approached the bedside, was deferential. The hand he extended in greeting was scrupulously clean.

Miss Dove gave him three fingers, like a duchess. "How d'y'do, Fred," she said. (She would have preferred to call him "Frederick" but he had not been christened so.) "You may be seated."

Fred sat on the edge of a chair. He placed his hat—a dark gray Homburg—upon his knees and folded his hands upon its crown.

Having nothing to say, Miss Dove waited for him to speak. She studied his face. She found it remarkably unchanged. It was a smooth face, neither good nor bad. There was no malice in it and very little character. The eyes, blue and cloudless as a child's, were set too wide apart.

Fred was, she knew, serving a sentence for forgery and the theft of an automobile, and so must be counted among her failures. But she did not blame herself. Rational humility had always told her that the ultimate success of a teacher depended, in some measure, upon the material with which she worked. In the last analysis one could not go behind the hand of Providence.

And yet, in Fred's case, it was possible that neither

she nor Providence had failed. Fred was a follower. When rules were made clear to him he obeyed them. It was only when he made independent choices— which an unrealistic society now forced him to make— that he invariably chose wrong. Miss Dove remembered how neat his margins had been and how he had always coughed in his handkerchief. She remembered also the offerings of fruit that he'd brought her each Friday—polished apples and tangerines and heavy bunches of Malaga grapes—until she'd discovered that he had stolen them from a grocer.

"I'm not over the hill," said Fred.

"I am gratified to hear that," said Miss Dove.

"When I seen in the paper you was sick I went to my gang-boss. 'Boss,' I says, 'the only teacher that ever learned me anything is in the hospital. I want a day off to go tell her I'm preparing to reform my ways.'"

"And he gave you leave?"

"Yes, ma'am. He says, 'Why sure, Fred. I know I can trust *you!*'"

"A compliment to cherish," said Miss Dove.

There was a tentative-sounding knock at the door and Geoffrey Lyon came in. In contrast to Fred's sober formality, his attire was loud and untidy. He wore brown flannels, a tweed jacket, a yellow shirt and a tattersall waistcoat. His shoes were rusty. One of them was untied. (He had often come to school improperly buttoned; Miss Dove remembered that.)

163

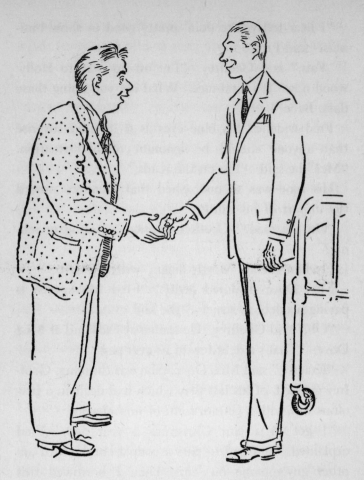

"Miss Dove," he said, "I'm Geoffrey Lyon."

"I know you, Geoffrey," said Miss Dove.

Fred jumped up. He grinned. "Recall the face, Geoff?" he asked.

Geoffrey whistled. "Old Babe Makepeace! The best slugger Cedar Grove ever had!"

"I hear tell you're doin' pretty good in show business," said Fred.

"Fair," said Geoffrey. "I'm on my way to Hollywood now. It's a rat-race. What are you doing these days, Babe?"

Fred widened his blue eyes as if in mild surprise that anyone should be ignorant of his situation. "Me?" he said. "I'm on the roads."

His tone was so unabashed that Geoffrey missed the import of his words.

"On the road?" Geoffrey queried. "Acting or selling?"

Fred laughed. "Mostly diggin' with a pick-ax."

Miss Dove deplored levity. "Fred Makepeace is paying his debt to society," she said.

"Oh," said Geoffrey. He smiled at Fred and at Miss Dove. "That's a debt few of us ever pay."

"Exactly," said Miss Dove. She was thinking, Geoffrey guessed, of his last play which had dealt in a frivolous way with a certain form of misbehavior.

"I got in a jam Christmas a year ago," Fred explained, "and had to pass a coupla checks with another guy's name on 'em. Then I borrowed this Chrysler from a parking lot and happened to wreck it."

"Tough," said Geoffrey.

"The judge woulda let me off with a fine and a suspended sentence," Fred said. "But I didn't know where to look for the money and I never did like probation. Makes me nervous."

"I can imagine," said Geoffrey.

"So I decided to pull my time and get it over with. I'm doin' twenty-four months on the roads."

"Fred was paroled for the day on his own recognizance," said Miss Dove.

"Splendid," said Geoffrey.

Billie Jean appeared. She was careful to look only at Geoffrey. "Your time is up, gentlemen," she said.

"Say! Aren't you little Billie McVay?" said Fred.

"I am Mrs. Green," Billie Jean said, without a glance in his direction.

"Well, pardon *me!*" said Fred.

Outside the hospital in the soft Spring air the two men chatted together.

"I guess you'll see a lot of cheese-cake in Hollywood," Fred said wistfully.

"It won't affect me," Geoffrey said. "I've got a B. W. and six kids in Upper Montclair."

"You don't say!" said Fred. "I had a wife but—" he laughed without the ring of pleasure "—like the feller says, she got away!" He sighed. "Well, I'd better start rollin'. I'm goin' back to the camp but to-day'll cost me time. I didn't have no parole. If I'd told the boss-man I wanted to see a sick teacher he'd of given me the horse laugh. I just laid down my pick and started walkin'."

"Where'd you get the Sunday clothes?"

"I borrowed 'em from a funeral home," Fred said.

"Well." A look of pain and wonder passed, like the drifting shadow of a cloud, across his face. "Did you notice how little she was?" he said. "Miss Dove, I mean."

Geoffrey nodded. "I noticed."

"Layin' in the bed not hardly bigger than a baby doll or a bird—one of them robins on the grass. If she had a husband he'd have to shake the sheets to find her. And I used to think she was Goliath."

"I know," said Geoffrey. He took out a pack of cigarettes. "Smoke?"

"Mind if I take two?" Fred asked. "One for the road."

"Take the pack," said Geoffrey.

"Thanks," Fred said. "Remember how we used to smoke in the boys' basement at Cedar Grove? Those were the days, Geoff. We'll never have it so good again!"

"Look, Babe," said Geoffrey. "When you—when they spring you, get in touch with me. I might be able to put you on to something."

"I'll do that thing," Fred said. "So long, boy. Give my regards to Marilyn Monroe."

Geoffrey watched his old schoolmate walk away. He noted how Fred hunched one shoulder as if to ward off a chilly wind. He felt creeping over him that mysterious mood of receptivity which is the courted darling of every artist. He knew, in his bones, how Fred felt and what had moved him to risk extra months of penal servitude for a brief visit to his lost childhood. He even understood himself—or almost. Why had he wanted Miss Dove with him when his first play appeared on Broadway? Sentimentality? Publicity? Ah, it had been more than that!

He looked, hardly seeing it—but *feeling* it, *feeling* it!—at the misty, low, tree-blurred skyline of Liberty Hill. In his mind a play had begun to take shape. It was the play he had always meant to write—a play woven of homespun human emotions like love and nostalgia and despair and fortitude. It was unlike the complicated, glittering things that had brought him fame. It was as simple as a Chekov!

Geoffrey tossed his cigarette into the gutter. He returned to his brother's house, went up to his room, locked the door, and put a sheet of paper on the roller of his portable typewriter. He started writing.

Once he cursed himself for being a literary leech who had no blood in his own veins and must batten upon the joys and sorrows of others. But the curse was lightly meant, and, in essence, happy. Geoffrey knew what kind of person he was; he wouldn't have changed if he could have. Soon his present surroundings—the chintzy guest-room with the hooked rugs and the botanical prints and the eiderdown quilts—had receded into oblivion. He was in another world. In it there was no sound but the dialogue of people in his mind and the steady tap-tapping of the keys.

At four-thirty or thereabout, Billie Jean began tidying the room. She whisked about rearranging objects
and flicking at imaginary dust in the immemorial fashion of a woman expecting important guests.

"Dr. Baker'll be here in a few minutes," she said.
"I want things prettied up."

Upon the bedside table she arranged a pitcher of
fresh ice-water, two clean glasses, and a stiff-backed
loose-leaf notebook. "That's your chart," she said.
"Everything's ready if he comes while I'm out. I'll
just slip down to the nurses' lounge a minute now."

So the waiting was nearly over, thought Miss Dove.
And suddenly the protective apathy she had assumed
fell away. Without the least compunction—and realiz-
ing perfectly the breach of hospital etiquette—she
reached for the notebook. She began to read her
chart.

She was not a self-conscious woman. She rarely
looked into a mirror and for many years she had been
too busy weighing her impressions of others to spec-
ulate upon their impression of her. Now, before her
fascinated gaze—neatly typed in the laconic, "un-pret-
tied-up" language of a medical man—was her own
image as reflected in the mind of Adams Temple.

"The patient," Dr. Temple had written, "is a slender, fully developed female aged fifty-five, showing few of the usual senile changes, lying quietly in bed in no apparent distress, alert and collected."

She read the sentence again. It was too long for style, she thought, but style had not been its author's object. It was grammatical. It was correctly punctuated. It was economically expressed. And as for the truth it conveyed—art could have done no better!

Billie Jean returned. She came and took the chart from Miss Dove's hands—*gently but firmly*, like a teacher confiscating a small boy's comic book. In her reproachful eyes was more sorrow than anger. "I'm surprised," she said. "I *trusted* you!"

"I'm sorry," said Miss Dove. But she was not sorry. The thing she had read had restored to her a sense of personal identity. Whatever tidings Thomas might bring she could receive as became a lady. Quietly, collectedly, and "in no apparent distress."

Thomas arrived accompanied by Mr. Porter.

The old gentleman refused a chair. "I can talk better on my feet," he said, "and I shan't stay long."

He stood leaning on his gold-headed cane, beetling his bushy brows, thrusting his pendulous underlip, and glaring at Miss Dove. The glare, Miss Dove knew, was a sign of that anger that is often, in the old and strong, a twin of pity. She despised pity. She rejected Mr. Porter's with a glance.

Thomas did not beat about the bush. "Surgery is indicated, Miss Dove," he said. "The sooner the better. And now—" he bowed to Mr. Porter.

"I am not here in a private capacity," said Mr. Porter, sounding unctuous in spite of his creaking voice. "I represent Rotary!"

"Indeed," said Miss Dove.

"Indeed, yes," said Mr. Porter. "Our chapter has voted unanimously to assume entire financial responsibility for the expenses of your illness."

Miss Dove opened her lips to speak. Mr. Porter silenced her.

"Wherever you choose to go for this operation," he said. "Rochester, Boston, Philadelphia, Baltimore—Rotary is behind you!"

"And if I decline the kind offer?" said Miss Dove.

A flush swept over Mr. Porter's gaunt face. He pounded his stick. "Who are you to decline it?" he demanded. "Who gave you the right to insult your friends? To walk the world with a haughty spirit—frightening little children, turning men to stone?"

"My dear sir," said Miss Dove, "if you wish my attention you must employ a civil tone. I am not to be bullied."

"Bullied!" Mr. Porter croaked. "*You* talk of bullying!" He turned to Thomas. "She's always been a stiff-necked termagant. Do you think *my* pride hasn't suffered, seeing the daughter of my friend penniless, working for her bread, wearing outlandish clothes—"

171

"You have forgotten yourself, Mr. Porter," said Miss Dove.

"I have forgotten nothing," Mr. Porter rejoined. "I haven't forgotten that I made you a *very* civil offer once!"

Mr. Porter had once offered Miss Dove his name. That had been fifteen years before when he had been a vigorous sixty-seven and a widower of a year's standing. He was rich. He was lonely. Miss Dove was undoubtedly lonely, too, and far from rich. What could have been more suitable?

Walking up Oakwood Street with a rose in his buttonhole and a spring in his gait he had felt utterly sanguine as to the success of his errand. He had been warmed by a glow of benevolence and armed with pretty phrases with which to soothe his lady-love when she would (as it didn't occur to him she wouldn't) droop against his broad chest with bird-like chirps of gratitude. And then she had refused him. She had simply said no, thank you, and changed the subject.

Now, in this hospital room, the chagrin of that old moment was plain as a wen on his face.

"The offer was generous," said Miss Dove, "but none-the-less ridiculous."

Mr. Porter trembled. His hawk's eyes blazed. But he knew he could not sustain his rage against Miss Dove. She had once done something for him, consciously or unconsciously, that would always command his devotion.

172

That had been in February '33, a black month that still recurred to him in dyspeptic nightmares. There had been a run on his bank. All morning the lobby had been packed and a line of frightened customers had moved toward the teller's window withdrawing the life-blood of trade. And then, bobbing among the milling, muttering throng, Mr. Porter saw the flat black hat and the pale pointed face of Miss Dove. Her features were composed. Only the tip of her nose was pinker than usual and that was owing, no doubt, to the frost in the air outside. She spoke. Her voice was not strident or even raised. It was the crisp, precise, level voice of the geography room at Cedar Grove School.

"Will you allow me passage, please," she said. "I wish to make a deposit."

She stared at the man at the head of the line—a man prepared to demand the last scrapings in the till —until, like one mesmerised, he stepped aside and allowed her to take his place. She deposited her salary check for the month. It was a check for ninety-eight dollars. She took her time. She did not slight those amenities that give grace to commerce in a small town. She inquired as to the state of Mr. Porter's health and, with particularity, into that of his wife, his cousins, his aunts and his nieces; she commented —and whether with irony or innocence he never knew—upon the flourishing business that the bank appeared to be doing. She had just completed her transaction when the courthouse clock struck three. Banking hours were over. Mr. Porter could close the teller's window, lower the green baize shade behind the glass, and put his head in his hands.

By next day the bank had been able to convert a few of its intangibles into ready cash but there had been, it transpired, no necessity for doing so. The temper of panic had passed.

Since then, whenever he had heard anyone speak of entertaining angels unaware, Mr. Porter had thought of Miss Dove.

"I am sure your Rotarians intended no offense," said Miss Dove, "but I am not an object of public charity."

"Insufferable woman!" Mr. Porter sputtered. "I knew what you were the day you were born. Those eyes! You got 'em from a taxidermist!"

The day she was born! Thomas looked at Miss Dove in wonder. Had she really come into the world naked and helpless as other infants came? (As Jincey's would come—but he had put anxiety resolutely aside.) The idea was fantastic. Crazy. Thomas had an impulse to hoot in the manner of conventional persons who are confronted suddenly with modern art.

But of course the ineluctable truth remained that even the terrible Miss Dove had begun life in the raw. She had been born in the orthodox fashion to the off-stage accompaniment of a more than orthodox fuss on the part of her male parent. Mr. Porter recalled the occasion with clarity.

He had set out for his office one fine morning in the autumn of 1896 when Jefferson, the Dove's colored butler, had stopped him. The doctor was with Mrs. Dove, Jefferson had said. The child was expected momentarily.

"Are things going badly?" Mr. Porter inquired in alarm.

"Not with Miss Betsy," Jefferson assured him. "But Mr. Phonnie! Oh, suh—he needs you!"

Mr. Porter had hurried to the house. There in the parlor he found his friend and saw at once that his condition was pitiable. Alphonzo Dove, ordinarily impeccably groomed, was clad in a pair of trousers over a flannel nightshirt, a red velvet smoking jacket, and carpet slippers embroidered by his wife in a design of pansies. His hair was a coxcomb. His elegant silken mustaches were pulled out of shape. His cheeks were unshaven. His eyes were wild.

"What can I do?" he gasped when he saw his visitor.

"Well, Phonnie," speculated Mr. Porter as his glance fell upon the brandy decanter that Jefferson had tactfully placed in full view upon the mantel, "I am told it helps to get drunk."

Alphonzo regarded him with horror. "Do you think me dead to decency?" he demanded. He groaned, covered his bloodshot eyes with his hands, and bowed

175

as if in prayer. "Drunk!" he whispered. "While above"—he lifted a forefinger toward the ceiling— "that bright saint of heaven descends the valley of the shadow?"

(And the extravagance of Mr. Dove's language should provoke in us no snide mistrust of his sincerity. Distraught as he was, the poor man spoke truly from a noble heart. It is a sad mistake, common to our cautious times, to assume that the expression of all valid feeling falls naturally into the monosyllabic or the vernacular.)

Alphonzo paced the Aubusson carpet. He stared out the window. He flung himself down upon sofas and chairs, rose, paced, flung himself down again. He stood in the middle of the room beneath the crystal chandelier and discoursed upon the grossness of all men and the purity of all women. He cursed himself for the sins of his bachelor days which—as Mr. Porter knew—had, in reality, been few and more akin to folly than to vice.

Mr. Porter, though his sympathies were aroused and the brandy that he sipped alone was excellent, found his friend's behavior trying.

"Hush, Phonnie," he said at last. "Listen!"

The walls were thick in that house and the doors were closed, but they could not entirely muffle the shrill, imperious clamor of life itself.

"Soprano or tenor?" said Mr. Porter.

Alphonzo made a dive for the door. Mr. Porter

blocked his way. "No you don't," he said. "You'll have to wait until you're sent for." He took Alphonzo by the hand, as he might have taken a child, and led him to a chair. "If all were not well they'd have told you."

After a short, but turbulent, interval of waiting, they were rewarded by the entrance of the doctor. Dr. Hurley—the original Dr. Hurley—was a dapper man with Gallic eyebrows and a step as brisk and light as that of a dancing master. He looked spruce, like an usher at a high-noon wedding. His face was as pink as the blanket bundle he carried in his arms.

"Betsy was a courageous girl and admirably equipped for her natural duty," he said. "You can see her presently, Phonnie. Meanwhile she sends you a pledge of her affection. A nice little daughter."

Alphonzo stared blankly.

"Will you accept it?" asked the doctor.

Alphonzo arose. Like a man coming in late to church he tiptoed to the doctor's side. He extended his arms, rigid as boards. The doctor laid his burden upon them.

A shiver went through Mr. Dove. His tension relaxed. His arms curved to a cradle, like a woman's arms.

Mr. Porter looked over his friend's shoulder. The baby was asleep. She was, of course, very small. Her face, folded shut, was an unlovely shade of red. Nobody could have guessed that here, wrapped in a blanket, was the public conscience of Liberty Hill!

Then she opened her eyes. They were not yet the cool, luminous gray eyes that were to freeze the marrow of sinners in Cedar Grove School. They were the eyes of the new-born—dark-blue, milky, and opaque. It was probably by accident that they seemed to focus, unflickering upon the eyes above them. But the expression in them was to endure. It was a steady look. A look of command. A look that made any man wish himself taller and straighter than he was. (Her father said afterwards that he was devoutly thankful he hadn't come to that first meeting with liquor on his breath!) Alphonzo bowed from the waist.

"Good morning, Miss Dove," he said.

Recalling that moment—so sentimental, so pretty, so buoyant with hope that had run out long ago—recalling his youth and his friend and his own child, the reckless, scapegrace son who had lived long enough to be killed at Bellau Wood—Mr. Porter felt all his fierceness desert him. He was only an old man leaning on a cane.

"It isn't charity that Liberty Hill offers you," he said gently. "It is—" He searched for a word that would satisfy her. Love? Gratitude? "It is Respect," he said.

"That," said Miss Dove with an air of *noblesse oblige*, "I shall accept with unqualified pleasure."

"Now," said Thomas, bringing the conversation back to medicine, "I've discussed your case with Dr. Hurley."

"What was young Dr. Hurley's opinion?"

"His opinion concurs with mine," Thomas said. "You have a small growth on your spine that must, if possible, be removed."

"If possible?"

"If possible," Thomas said. "Until we go in we can never be sure about the nature of any tumor."

"Oh," said Miss Dove. She understood. She was not so naive as to fail to guess the word the doctor had chosen not to use.

"All you have to decide," said Mr. Porter, "is *who* shall remove it and where!"

"Aren't you competent?" Miss Dove asked Thomas.

"Yes," Thomas said without hesitation. "I am." (Miss Dove liked men who did not pretend to diffidence.) "But there are surgeons with more experience and reputation. And I am not a Boards man."

He explained that he had not yet taken certain examinations which would qualify him as a Fellow of the American Board of Surgeons. He had completed the residency in a celebrated teaching hospital and had expected to be examined, but financial considera-

179

tions had altered his plans. When he had been offered a staff-position in the new hospital in Liberty Hill he had felt obligated to accept it at once. His parents had other sons to educate.

"I plan to take Boards this summer," he said. "But in the meantime—"

"I am not a Boards *woman,*" said Miss Dove.

This was true. Miss Dove had not satisfied the state Board of Education's requirements for a grade-A certificate. She had never had a course in educational psychology or classroom management. She was rated —and paid—as a sub-standard teacher.

"If you decide to go elsewhere that won't be interpreted by anyone as a reflection upon my ability," Thomas said. "The operation is extremely delicate."

"The club can charter a plane," said Mr. Porter. "There's a famous man at the Mayo Clinic—"

"Allow me to deliberate," said Miss Dove.

Mr. Porter leaned on his cane. Billie Jean stood, still as a statue, against the wall. Thomas waited at the foot of the bed. His hands rested lightly upon the rail.

Miss Dove deliberated. Her thoughts took her far into the past.

She was in the geography room. The third grade was painting maps. There was quiet in the room except for the occasional faint musical clink of a paintbrush striking the edge of a glass. Miss Dove reached for a book. As she did so she upset a box of chalk.

She was mortified by the accident; she had never done such an awkward thing before.

It was a new box, scarcely broached. Its contents spilled on the floor behind the teacher's desk making a rattling sound, like a shower of pebbles. The pupils looked up. Their hands shot into the air. They were

all bright-faced, glad of diversion, eager to be of help.

"You may continue painting," Miss Dove told them distantly. "I can attend to this."

To retrieve the chalk she squatted down, balancing

her modest derriere upon her heels. She was thankful that her solid-front desk hid her from view for she thought a stooping position incongruous with dignity. She was arranging the sticks of chalk neatly in the box, lining them up as they'd been packed originally, when she sensed an electric quality in the silence of the room. Then something soft brushed her cheek, her neck. It fell about her shoulders. It was her hair!

Pivoting on the balls of her feet she came face to face with Thomas Baker. He held one wire hairpin between his thumb and forefinger. Half a dozen others protruded from his mouth.

For an awful moment she glimpsed ignominious defeat. The citadel of her privacy, of her immutability, had been invaded by an eight-year-old boy! She would soon be an object of derision. She wanted to shake Thomas until his bones rattled, until he choked on the hairpins.

Happily, however, an expedient occurred to her. If he was dexterous enough to remove the pins without her knowledge, he was dexterous enough to repair his mischief!

She spoke in an almost inaudible whisper close to Thomas' blushing ear. "Put each one back in its proper place," she said, and turned away to continue gathering up the chalk.

Her appearance, when she resumed her throne, was quite usual. Her face was impassive. Her hair was

182

screwed into its customary knot at the nape of her neck.

"Remember to print your names legibly in the lower right hand corners of your margins," she had said to the class.

She had not glanced at Thomas.

Now, twenty years later, she did glance at him.

"I remember," she said, "that you had very skillful fingers."

"You had very pretty hair, Miss Dove," said Thomas.

Miss Dove did not smile. She never smiled except in a perfunctory way—a mere turning up of the corners of her thin lips—at PTA parties in the school cafeteria. But for an instant her face softened.

"I shall feel perfectly safe," she said, "in the hands of my children."

It was too much for old Mr. Porter. Wheezing back his tears, he stumped out of the room. Billie Jean followed him with a glass of water.

"Now that the air is clear of emotion," said Miss Dove to Thomas, "we can resume our discussion."

"I think we ought to do it Saturday," Thomas said. "Tomorrow. As you used to tell us, there is no merit in delay."

"None," said Miss Dove. "Tomorrow, then."

"Shall I notify your sisters?"

"Afterwards," she said.

"As you wish," said Thomas. At ten that evening, he told her, she would swallow a capsule containing a powerful soporific. She would sleep soundly. So soundly that next morning when she was given a hypodermic she might scarcely know—certainly, she wouldn't care. She would be taken to the operating room and put under general anesthesia. Because of the position of her tumor the operation for its removal would be slow. It might be lengthy. In that event, the anesthetic would be prolonged and so would its after-effects. It might well be Sunday before she really awoke.

"Where?" asked Miss Dove.

"What?"

"Where will I awake?"

Thomas shook his head. The Bakers, Miss Dove recalled, had never been good at dissembling.

"I don't know, Miss Dove," he said.

Miss Dove, as her history would bear out, was little given to swagger. But even she was not proof against

184

that human vanity which impels one to say something memorable and gallant upon the eve of crisis.

"Here or there is immaterial," she said, with a shrug in her voice. "I have long been curious about the topography of Heaven."

Later, she reflected that the boast had been unworthy of her. It was unworthy because it was untrue. She took a rather cool view of Heaven.

She did not question the existence of that far bourne. It lay, she presumed, beyond all the horizons and solar systems and galaxies that the finite mind of man could imagine. It was an estimable country. But from hearsay, the contours of its land, the character of its fauna, and the aspect of its populace did not appeal to her. There were too many sheep there. (Silly creatures!) Golden streets were ostentatious. Rivers that flowed with milk and honey would attract flies. Faces "shining as the sun" sounded hard on the eyes. And the place held no room for improvement! Its institutions and inhabitants were perfect. How dull it would be for a teacher!

Naturally, Miss Dove had never voiced that objection. (Criticism of orthodox beliefs she considered vulgar and jejune and harmful to the masses.) She hardly knew she entertained it. Heaven was her eventual home. She would be loyal to it. Someday she would go there and accept, with what grace she could muster, beatific and perpetual idleness.

Only—she whispered to herself—not tomorrow!

Pretending to read a magazine, she thought of the places—the lowly, earthbound places—that she did long to see. They ran through her mind like snatches of poetry. The white cliffs of Dover, the Lake Country, and all the green English countryside. Paris. Rome on its Seven Hills. Rivers and deltas and black forests where bull elephants charged through the undergrowth and supple feline animals stalked their prey. The Orient. The Arctic Circle. The Northwest Passage? In Miss Dove's childhood that short route from east to west, though a lost cause to explorers, had still stirred the young with adventurous hope. She had planned to discover it herself when she grew up and the plan had never ceased haunting her.

How small and circumscribed her life had been! She had a great yearning to burst its bounds—to see, to admire, to be free!

"The day's beginning to fade," said Billie Jean. She turned on the lamp.

Supper was over. Nurses were changed. Jincey looked in again—paler this time, but still undiscouraged. Will I ever see the child? Miss Dove asked herself. Will I know whether it's a boy or girl?

There was much she wanted to know. After her retirement she had meant to study Greek and geology.

She had meant to learn more about the migratory habits of birds. She regretted neglecting to verify the statement about the flavor of ants that Angela had queried long ago.

Dr. Temple came to listen to her chest. Mere hospital busy-work, Miss Dove thought impatiently; but recalling his description of herself, she was gracious to him.

"When you write to your mother, which I trust you do at regular intervals—" she began.

"Once a week," he said.

"You may tell her I do not find you unastute."

"She'll be proud to hear that," he said. "*She's* so keen that she sometimes fancies her family more obtuse than it is!"

"Do you know how ants taste?" Miss Dove asked without preamble, simply because she suddenly burned to know.

The nurse looked alarmed (was the patient wandering?) and Miss Dove herself was aware that the question had a mildly lunatic ring.

But Adams Temple—Angela's own true son!—was a young man to whom curiosity, per se, seemed a normal, wholesome appetite.

"Why, yes. My mother told me," he said. "She ate one once, when she was a little girl. They taste like sour pickles."

Fearing to unhinge her patient's mind even further, the nightnurse was more silent than usual. She sat

187

buffing her fingernails (a boudoir rite, Miss Dove reflected, that no person of refined instinct would perform in company) and casting occasional wary glances in the direction of the bed. When the Reverend Mr. Burnham appeared she was visibly relieved.

"I'll leave you with your pastor," she said and discreetly withdrew.

Alexander laid a prayerbook on the table and sat down in a chair close to the bed.

This visit, Miss Dove thought, was the final test of her power of humility. It had been hard to accept

Thomas as a medical authority and harder to preserve equanimity beneath the stethoscope of young Temple and the bossy ministrations of Billie Jean. To regard Alexander Burnham as her spiritual shepherd was hardest of all.

In church she found it easy. There the familiar rhythm of the service, the candles and the organ and the vestments combined to give him a kind of exalted anonymity. He seemed less a man than a symbol of office and quite dissociate from the high-strung boy who had been a touchy problem in Cedar Grove School.

He had been an uncertain child. Too tense. Too much enamoured of magnificence to endure willingly the long stretches of mediocrity that lie between the peaks of experience. And he had been afraid. Miss Dove had done what she could. She had tried to show him that he was not unique, that—in her room at least —he was subject only to the strict but unfrightening laws of cause and effect. Once she had protected him. But from another. Not from himself.

One day a pane of glass in the window of the principal's office had been broken. After recess a baseball was found among the shattered glass on the floor. Around it in an equatorial band the name "Alexander the Great" was printed in old English script.

The principal, who liked to impose discipline in a delayed and pompous way, had waited until school was out to question the suspect. He had chosen the geography room—possibly because its climate was unfriendly to falsehood—as the scene of his inquisition. Miss Dove had sat at her desk, divorcing herself from the proceedings while her so-called superior—a man of coarser grain than Mr. Spivey—had confronted Alexander with his evidence.

"Is this your ball, Sandy?" he asked, striding down the aisle to the spot where the accused child stood.

Alexander glanced at the ball. He blenched. "Yes, sir," he said.

"You positively identify it?"

"Yes, sir." A greenish tinge crept into the boy's pallor.

The principal gave him a menacing look. "You're

guilty of destroying school property, aren't you?"

Alexander swallowed. Miss Dove could see the muscle bulging in his throat as he struggled with himself. "No, sir," he said.

"You deny that you broke the window?"

"No," said Alexander. "I mean yes. I didn't break it."

The principal gave vent to a cynical laugh. "Now look, Sandy. Don't give me that guff! We all know you never let anyone else touch that ball. We—"

Miss Dove spoke. Her voice was controlled and quiet and incisive as a new-honed blade.

"The child has answered you," she said. "You asked your question. He gave you his word."

"But—" the principal began.

"There are no 'buts,'" she said. She fixed her terrible calm eyes upon the flustered man. "The incident is closed."

The principal thumped the baseball down upon the teacher's desk. "Very well," he said as he left the room, "*you* manage it!"

"I will," said Miss Dove.

For a moment Alexander stood where he was, trembling, turning greener. Then he lunged forward. He reached the sink in the corner by the sand-table. He gripped its sides and bent over it retching again and again.

Miss Dove did not go to him to hold his head or wipe his mouth with a cool damp rag. She sat on at her desk, as if he did not exist, and heard him try in vain to vomit up his lie.

When, at last, he was quiet, she said: "Remember to take your baseball as you go."

Now he was a man. A man to whom other men came for advice in perplexity. A man useful in church and state. He was one of her successes, she supposed; but it was difficult to forget the boy at the sink, the boy whose name in the Book had been followed by a rare symbol—a question mark! And yet, in simple parochial duty, she must forget him now.

"Thomas has told you?" said Miss Dove.

"That he'll operate tomorrow? Yes," said Alexander. "I'm glad you're staying here. Tommy's as good as they come."

"The outcome is doubtful," she said.

"All outcomes are. Always," said Alexander.

"I do not wish to die," said Miss Dove. Now she had said it. She had used the word. She felt curiously purged.

"No. Of course not," he agreed. "It may seem strange, in view of my calling, but I do scorn the person who is resigned to death. He is ungrateful to life."

"Life—" said Miss Dove. She dwelt on the word as on a lover's name. "It is—" But she had not the eloquence to say what it was. "I have been happy," she said.

She had never said so before. She had, in fact, considered it ignoble to measure euphoria. She saw now that she had been one of the blessed simply because she had not guessed she was.

"I know," said Alexander.

"Thomas is not hopeful, is he?" she asked.

"Not very," said Alexander. "But there is a hope that transcends the medical!" He reached for the prayerbook. "Perhaps if we read from this—"

Miss Dove was grateful for his candor. She repaid it now in kind.

"Do you intend to read the general confession?" she asked.

He nodded. "In such circumstances that is customary."

"Then I must warn you," she said, "that when I repeat that prayer I do so with reservations."

"Reservations?"

"Yes," she said. "I have made mistakes. I have my human limitations. But I do not, in all honesty, find the burden of my sins intolerable. And I haven't erred and strayed like a sheep!"

"The language is archaic, I'll grant you," Alexander said. "But it contains the core of truth. All of us—"

But Miss Dove was adamant. "No," she said. "I have never spoken hypocrisy to my Maker and now is scarcely a propitious moment to begin." Her neck, propped on the pillow, looked very stiff indeed. "I am not 'a miserable offender.' "

The rector smiled. His smile was warm and engaging and bright with the good gaiety that radiates from men whose hearts are leavened by work they love. Why, Miss Dove thought, he is at ease with himself. He is the man I wished him to become.

"And I'll tell you a secret, Miss Dove," he said. "Neither am I!"

He sat with her for a while, there in the hospital room that was as small and nearly as ascetic as a monk's cell. He talked of the world outside—of his garden where the crocuses were up, of the old gnarled crabapple that was in full bud in the courthouse square and of the foreign places he had seen as a chaplain in the navy. Just before he left he said casually, almost in the manner of after-thought: "We could have our prayer now if you like. Silently, but together."

"I *should* like," said Miss Dove.

She could not know—nor did she try to guess—the nature of Alexander's petition, but her own was simple. "Whatever comes to me," she pleaded, "let me take it like a Teacher!"

The nurse came in. She carried a saucer upon which a yellow capsule reposed in one of those little fluted paper cups that usually contain chocolate creams.

Miss Dove swallowed the capsule.

After the lamp was out she lay waiting for sleep to

trip her in the thoughts, gazing at the square of
sky framed in the window. The sky was a deep,
stained-glass blue and perfectly clear except for one
long, thin line of transparent cloud. Over it innumer-
able stars seemed to swim and swirl like a swarm of
crystal bees. Then, as if Miss Dove had stepped aside
at a remove from actuality, she saw her own star—the
planet Earth, her darling, which she knew in all its
beauty and imperfection—hung aloft outside her window. It was no bee. No trivial celestial insect. It was
a round ball as large as the globe on her schoolroom
desk. It glowed with a brilliance that came not from
without but from within, and it revolved slowly so
that she could see the familiar patterns of its conti-
nental bodies shadowed on its surface. She had done
what she could for it. Now, like a child just graduated
from Cedar Grove, it was on its own—beyond her care
or correction. She bade it godspeed as it spun in the
April night.

On Saturday morning at eight o'clock Dr. Baker
stood in the corridor outside the operating rooms and
talked with his interne, Dr. Temple. He appeared relaxed, unhurried, and steady of nerve which, as a matter of fact, he was. Just before an operation—no
matter how difficult or fraught with danger—this miraculous thing always happened to him. Tranquility

descended upon his spirit. Cares fell away from his mind and left it clean and sharp like a scalpel.

"The parson and the cop are in the lobby," Adams Temple said. "Potential blood donors. They both match."

"Good," said Thomas. He lit a cigarette. His hand did not shake.

"An odd pair," Adams said.

"Oh, I don't know. They both grew up here in Liberty Hill. They went to the same school."

"I talked a bit with the cop," Adams said. "He told me about his life—sketchily of course. How he pulled himself up by his bootstraps with Miss Dove's moral aid. A remarkable story."

"Bill's quite a guy," Thomas said absently.

"If he does give her a transfusion," Adams went on, "or even if he doesn't—just because he's here ready to—and this thing turns out well it will mean a lot to him. To all of you."

"You're damn right it will," said Thomas.

"Psychologically, I mean," Adams explained. "A sort of rounding out of the cycle of maturity."

Thomas smoked in silence. At the moment he wanted nothing less than to be forced into introspection. This bright, pontifical lad got on his nerves.

But Adams continued to worry his thesis. "It's like the pious Aeneas turning back into burning Troy," he said. "Remember? He took the old Anchises—his own father—on his shoulders and bore him, like a child, away from the flames."

"I follow your drift," said Thomas drily. "But I lack your classical background."

"Well," Adams told him. "*My* Miss Dove taught Latin."

Thomas tossed his cigarette into a jardiniere filled with sand. "It's time to scrub," he said. "You ought to be a psychiatrist."

"I think I shall be," Adams said. "What's surgery but sublimated butchery?"

If Adams had been a permanent interne instead of a temporary whose place would be hard to fill, Thomas might have fired him on the spot. Instead, he only laughed. "At least we don't plug our patients into the wall," he said lightly.

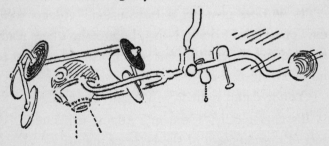

The operation lasted for hours. During the morning a number of callers came to the hospital. There was nothing they could do, they knew. They were drawn there, as by a magnet, to enquire, to leave their cards, and go away.

John Wesley Evans buttonholed the Reverend Mr. Burnham. He spoke feelingly of his personal reformation.

"It was like Damascus," he declared. "I'll never touch another drop!"

Alexander, who was ordinarily impatient of John Wesley's ups and downs, spoke kindly.

"Take it easy, Wes," he advised. "A day at a time."

For the most part, Billie Jean remained in her patient's empty room. Now and then, however, just for the pure pleasure of gazing on William Holloway who sat, majestic and muscular, in a brown leather lounge chair—she found an excuse for consulting the receptionist in the lobby. She was there when the delegation from Cedar Grove School arrived.

The delegation was composed of four girls and eight boys. Their faces, preternaturally clean, were solemn, brave, and scared. The girls were in Brownie dresses and the boys in Cub Scout uniforms. Their right sleeves were rolled to their shoulders.

Billie Jean met them at the door.

"Children aren't allowed without their parents," she said. "What do you want?"

"We're on important business," young David Burnham said haughtily. "A matter of life or death."

"Let me talk," said Vicky Evans. "I'm spokesman."

"Okay, big shot," said David.

"We came to give blood to Miss Dove," said Vicky. She crooked out her bare arm as if expecting to be seized and bled on the instant. She bit her lips and squinched her eyes shut.

David shoved her. "Dope! They don't do it out here. They lay you down and afterwards they give you tomato juice."

"We don't do it anywhere to folks your age," said Billie Jean.

"We're all big," piped a diminutive, pigtailed girl. "We're all over nine!"

"We have health badges," said Vicky. "Our blood's *strong!*"

Billie Jean's maternal tenderness was touched. "Listen, honeys," she said gently, "we don't need you. We've got David's daddy and Officer Holloway right here. But I know something you *can* do for Miss Dove."

"What?" asked David suspiciously, as if he knew the project would be dull.

"The proficiency test's Monday," said Billie Jean. "If she comes back to school and finds you flunked it she'll be good and mad! She'll be *terrible!* You go home and study for that!"

"Heck," someone muttered. "We know that junk!"

"Are you sure?" asked Billie Jean. In rapid succession she pointed her finger at child after child, firing questions like bullets. "What's the difference between longitude and latitude? Name the Great Lakes. The chief product of Brazil. Where is the Tropic of Capricorn?"

At each shot the children backed nearer to the door. At last they were gone.

"You managed that like a seasoned diplomat, Billie Jean," said Alexander.

Billie Jean smiled. "I wish I knew the answers!" She dabbed at her eyes. "Those cute little tykes," she murmured brokenly and hurried away.

Holloway cleared his throat. The courage of the children had moved him and Billie Jean's tears he considered womanly and genteel.

The children trailed along the sidewalk looking up at the hospital windows.

"That's where she is," said David. "That top room at the corner."

"No. That's where ladies have babies," one of his companions objected.

"Davie's right," said Vicky. "I was in there when I had my tonsils out. It's all tiled, like a bathroom. They put you on a table under a huge light and make you blow up a balloon."

"That's the ether," said David.

They stared. They tried to imagine the terrible Miss Dove lying on a table in a bathroom, puffing at a balloon. The effort was beyond them. On a common impulse they scampered off to a vacant lot where they played kick-the-can until their spirits rose so high that David called Vicky an ugly name which she, quite properly, resented. Later in the day, however, she wrote him a poem in which she told him he was her knight in armor and she was sorry she had kicked him in the stomach.

Meanwhile Miss Dove had set out on a very grand tour.

Precisely when the journey began (was it when Miss Dove had her vision of the home planet?) and how long it lasted and what ground it covered are questions impossible to answer. Even Miss Dove was baffled by them. Now and then she would find herself in a new place without knowing how she had got there and she would move on before she had a chance to clarify her recollections. She decided that as soon as she arrived at her destination—whatever that might be—she would sit down quietly in a room alone and fill in the gaps in her memory. She was not fond of gaps.

The truth is that she knew all there was to know.

She had entered a realm where ordinary laws—the laws of gravity and space and time—are not constant.

At first she was being carried—in a palanquin she presumed—across a beautiful plain that spread out on either side and was dotted with clusters of buildings. Pagodas. Palaces. Temples. Bells were ringing in the distance—they made a mellow, wistful sound—and the colors of the landscape were clear and delicate. The trees had twisted trunks and their spreading, wind-flattened crowns were a soft sea-green outlined in gold. They were like the trees in a Chinese tapestry. Beneath one tree a man stood reading a book. He wore a crimson gown and a long, thin chin-beard that fell to his knees.

"Are you Marco Polo?" he called when he saw Miss Dove.

"No," she replied, finding nothing strange in his question. "I am Miss Dove of Liberty Hill!"

"Miss Dove!" he cried and made a deep obeisance.

Why, this is old Cathay! she thought. Of course. She saw now that the whole plain was encircled by a wall. She wished to explore it thoroughly—to go into its temples and its fabulous gardens and to talk to its wise men so she could tell her father all about it.

She didn't know the language of the palanquin bearers but she remembered that French was the international tongue. What was the French for "Stop"? All she could think of was "Parlez-vous Français" which did not sound right. "Attention, please!" she said in a distinct tone. But even as she spoke she saw that the scene had changed. She must have crossed the wall without noticing.

She was in the middle of a desert.

Suddenly she realized that she was not riding in a palanquin. She was sitting on a seat made of four joined hands which belonged to Thomas Baker and Alexander Burnham. The boys were grinning up at her in an impish way. They were about eleven years old. They wore red sweaters and corduroy knickers. Alexander was smoking a cigarette.

"How unseemly!" she said. "Put me down at once."

Thomas wiggled his ears. "This is *my* theatre of command," he said.

"You have never been in more grievous error," said Miss Dove. "Put me down."

"Keep your spine rigid," said Thomas. "Ready, Sandy? One—two—three—*go!*"

Instead of putting her down they swung her aloft. She left their hands and bounced into the air—very lightly, she remarked, like a soap-bubble—and found herself perched comfortably upon the hump of a camel.

The camel half-turned its head and looked at her with one mournful eye. "I'm not a pretty beast," it said.

Miss Dove was chagrined. Although she had dictated those words many times to the advanced first grade, she would never have been so unfeeling as to say them to a camel's face.

"Pretty is as pretty does," she said.

"I can go many days without water," the camel said. It moved off toward the flat, treeless horizon.

Miss Dove was agreeably surprised at the smoothness of its gait. She had understood that the motion of a camel was apt to be jerky and rough, but this one seemed to glide. He was, indeed, a veritable "ship of the desert." She felt borne along on a gently undulating stream.

Elaine the fair, Elaine the lovable,

Miss Dove the grim, Miss Dove the terrible—the lines flowed drowsily through her mind. She shook them off.

The desert looked exactly like the sand-table desert that the third grade always made when it was introduced to Arabia. Only, of course, no table could begin to suggest this sense of illimitable space, of vastness and emptiness stretching beyond the scope of the eye or the imagination. Then, against the horizon, she saw a caravan. Its "desert ships" and their robed riders were purple. They might have been cut from the purple cardboard that the children used to suggest distance.

Miss Dove and her steed were approaching an oasis. It was a green, inviting spot—a clump of date palms around a bubbling spring.

"Could you take a sip of water?" asked the camel. His voice was like a woman's voice, soft and wheedling. "Just a little sip of water?"

Miss Dove was tempted. She would have enjoyed a sip. But pride would not permit her to be less abstemious than a beast.

"We will wait until big recess," she said.

Before long she regretted her refusal. Her mouth was dry. When, shimmering near at hand, she saw another clump of palms, she said she would now like to pause for refreshment.

"That one is a mirage," the camel said contemptuously. "You can go thirsty."

"You must employ a civil tone," said Miss Dove.

The camel snorted. It turned its head to her. Its heavy-lidded eye, its curling lips and its long yellow teeth made her think of Mr. Porter. "I made you a civil offer once," it said.

When the desert was crossed, how she dismounted from her perch, Miss Dove could not say. She only knew that before long she was in an airplane speeding over land and sea and receiving a kaleidoscope of impressions that were both strange and familiar.

The plane was not like the big liner in which, at Geoffrey Lyon's invitation, she had flown to New York. It was such a machine as she had watched rise above the county fairgrounds in the summer of 1910.

She flew it herself. She sat in an open cockpit and held the stick with one hand while with the other she pressed down hard on the crown of her hat to prevent its blowing off.

It was night. The moon and stars were shining. They were very close to her or else her vision was even more acute than usual. She saw the craters on the moon and the rings around Saturn and the seventh star in the Pleiades. For an instant she let her hat take its chances while she reached out and nearly touched the Southern Cross. Below her, white in the moonlight, gleamed the remnants of antiquity—the leaning tower, the pyramids, the broken columns of the Parthenon. Black ink-blots of jungle were spilled, sprawling, over the earth; in their depths she saw the burning jewel eyes of tigers on the prowl and the great rivers winding silver to the sea. The Ganges. The Euphrates. The Nile. She knew each one by its peculiar bends and turns that she had so often traced on the schoolroom map. The sea itself. The vast, mysterious matrix of all life. Wider than the desert. Wide as the sky.

Near her some invisible person was singing an old, silly song that made her think of honeysuckle at a dormitory window.

"Come take a ride in my ai-rr-plane

And we'll vis-it the man in the moon!"

Miss Dove sniffed. "The moon is a dead planet," she said. "A satellite of the Earth. Because of its intense cold and the lack of oxygen in its atmosphere it cannot support any form of life, animal or vegetable."

"Yes, Miss Dove," a voice replied.

The plane nosed downward. It went into a spin. Round and round and round and round into a funnel of darkness went Miss Dove. She lay fathoms deep in water. Slowly, she floated upward. She had an impression of light seeping down upon her. She had nearly reached the surface. She had reached it. There was an odor of flowers and of something else—half sweet, half sickening—pulling her down. Faces bent above her. If they would go away, move back, give her air—

She was in Paris. The chestnuts were in flower. Ladies, exquisitely gowned, strolled beside handsome gentlemen with mustaches like her father's. Well-mannered children sailed boats on a pond. Everything was suave and *comme il faut* and yet she was uneasy. Paris was a beautiful city full of beautiful names— Champs d'Élysées, Bois de Boulogne, Place de la Concorde—but she did not trust it. She would have

207

liked to buy a book at one of the stalls along the Seine but she didn't dare lest it be an improper one. She was still thirsty but she was afraid to sit at a table at a sidewalk cafe and order a drink lest the waiter—the *garçon*—should bring her something alcoholic.

" 'Oh to be in England, now that April's here'!" she sighed.

"It's just past the channel," said a man at her elbow. Or did he say "crisis?" He had an American accent—a Liberty Hill accent. "It ought to be smooth sailing."

"Thank you," said Miss Dove. She descended a flight of rickety steps to a pier at the end of which a small steamship was bobbing on choppy water. The man called down to someone on the ship.

"She's all right," he called. "Let her sleep!"

Let her sleep, let her sleep, let her sleep—

In London she felt more at home. A bobby saluted her. "They're expecting you, mum," he said. He put her into a cab—a hansom cab—and she rode through the gray calm heart of London past the British Museum and Trafalgar Square and The Old Curiosity Shop. Big Ben struck the hour. The bells of St. Paul's and St. Ive's chimed together. The cab stopped at the gates of Buckingham Palace. Miss Dove alighted. A soldier in a busby flung open the gate. "They're expecting you," he said.

Miss Dove went past him. A garden party was in progress. Among the guests Miss Dove spotted her mother who was dressed in black but carrying a pink silk parasol that cast rosy light upon her face and made it look young and debonair. She smiled at her daughter and continued talking gaily to a little page.

Miss Dove sat down at a round table. Presently Queen Mary joined her. The queen's manner was stately and affable. She wore a high turban covered with feathers and violets. She exuded an agreeable odor of lavendar.

"Miss Dove," she said, "I admire your hat."

"Thank you, ma'am," said Miss Dove, congratulating herself upon remembering to say 'ma'am' to the Queen. "It is not to be compared with yours. *Yours* is a *chapeau.*"

Her Majesty stroked the feathers on her hat. "I always wash before applying scent," she said. "Would you care to see my herbaceous border?"

"Indeed, yes," said Miss Dove who was an amateur of botany.

At a respectful distance she followed her hostess. But she never saw the border. Instead, when she came to the end of the path she found herself standing on the jutting point of a cliff at the edge of a high plateau. Far below—so far that looking down made her dizzy—a narrow inlet joined two great seas that lay to left and right. Between the promontory upon which she stood and another promontory exactly like hers, a footbridge spanned the chasm. It was a flimsy-looking bridge made of wire and barrel staves and less than a yard in width. Miss Dove drew back.

"Is it London Bridge?" she asked.

"It's condition is satisfactory," said the Queen. "It's only the Northwest Passage."

"Of course," said Miss Dove. The aurora borealis spread its giant fan of colors on the sky. Far down in the water an iceberg reflected the colors and sailed serenely out to sea like a great cumulous cloud full of the setting sun.

At the further end of the bridge stood the young archeologist. He wore white flannel trousers, a dark blue blazer, a high collar and a stiff straw hat which he removed with a flourish.

"Do you know *me*, Miss Dove?" he asked and his voice, though familiar, sounded different from the voice of the young man she had talked to on the campus lawn. "I'm rather bizarre, but quite benign!"

Miss Dove crossed the bridge. She walked gingerly at first but by the time she reached the middle she had no fear of falling. On the other side of the chasm the world was bathed in pellucid gold. All the vegetation was overlaid with a patina of light. Each lacquered blade of grass stood separate from its neighbor. On every leaf on every tree the delicate vein-structure was visible.

The air had a new quality. As Miss Dove drew it into her lungs she was filled with a desire to dance, to sing, to laugh. To loosen her hair and let it blow in the wind. She had discovered, she felt, some marvelous secret that prompted the pulse of the universe.

"Under these happy auspices—" the young archeologist began and would have seized her hand.

She darted away from him.

"I must tell them!" she cried. "I must tell them!"

Once she looked back to see if he were following, but he was only standing there, decorous and unimportunate.

She ran through the town of Liberty Hill. William Holloway stared, shocked and disillusioned, as she passed him at Maple and Grant. He raised a big gloved paw to halt her. She did not halt.

She ran down the central corridor of Cedar Grove School. Mr. Spivey was standing just outside his office. His bald head was a wan day-moon in the dim academic light.

She took a long, flying leap and slid along the floor, as she had seen boys do when they thought she wasn't looking. She slid straight to the geography room and in at the door.

The room was noisy and bright with children. They were playing leap-frog over the desks. They sang and shouted and called one another rude names. The shirttails of the boys flapped behind them. The skirts of the girls belled out, blue and pink and yellow and lilac, like flowers of the field.

When they saw Miss Dove they reined in their joy. They went to their seats. They opened their notebooks and sat erect—feet on the floor, hands folded on the desks, solemn eyes to the front.

Miss Dove mounted the platform. "Attention, please," she said. She meant her voice to ring, but it came out level and precise. She wanted to say to the children: "Unclasp your little hands! Forget the rules. A fig for margins!" She wanted to tell them: "Look for the golden light and the new-veined leaf! Drink the air of Spring! Life is the only thing that matters at all. Life!"

But the spell that had fallen upon the class fell upon her. She could not speak. The only sound in the room was that of a fly buzzing against a screen. She picked up yesterday's folded newspaper, which she had saved against such an emergency. At a measured pace she walked to the window and swatted the fly.

"The Alps, I presume," said Miss Dove to the young archeologist. She was in a meadow where young goats with bells on their collars tumbled among flowers and filled the air with tinkling clatter. She pointed to a range of mountains.

"Yes. In a manner of speaking," he said. "And beyond lies—"

She did not wait to hear what lay beyond. She began to climb. Like a mountain goat she leapt from crag to crag. She was amazed at her own agility.

But when, with her companion puffing behind her, she reached what she thought must surely be the summit of the mountain, she found she was mistaken. It was only an upland pasture, a resting place, above which the true peak ascended, glassy with ice and too steep for any foot, goat or human. From the apex of the peak stretched a steel cable down which slid a little car—a kind of basket, really, like those beneath balloons at expositions.

Alphonzo Dove stepped out of the basket. "I came down to meet you, dear child," he said. "How did you stand the trip?"

"Very well, thank you, sir," said Miss Dove. She was glad to see her father, but not at all surprised. He wore a green alpine-climbing costume. A sprig of eidelweiss was stuck into the band of his hat. An old brown vellum-bound book peeped from the pocket of his jacket. His jaunty mustaches glittered in the sun.

"You go the rest of the way by funicular," he said with a gesture toward the basket. "Don't be afraid. It's rather bizarre, but quite benign."

Bizarre. Benign. Miss Dove started. Someone else had said that. Someone else dressed in green. She turned her head.

"What are you looking for?" Alphonzo asked.

"For Thomas Baker," said Miss Dove.

"The child with the ears," said Alphonzo.

"Oh," said the archeologist, "he's not a Boards man. Are you a Boards woman?"

"No," said Miss Dove, "but I have passed my proficiency test."

"She's in no apparent distress," said her father, "though her hair is rather bizarre."

Bizarre, benign. Benign, bizarre. Bizarre, bizarre, bz-z-z-z.

She was in the funnel again. She was under water. She was floating. She was coming up—up—up—

She opened her eyes.

She was lying, of course, in her hospital bed. Beside her stood a tall iron contraption, like a floor lamp, that held a jar of clear liquid. From the bottom of the jar depended a small rubber tube that was attached by a needle to the vein in the inside bend of her elbow. Glucose, she thought correctly and knew where she was and what had happened.

From outside, beyond glass, she heard the court-house clock striking the half, and then the sweet, dissonant ringing of churchbells. It was Sunday. Those were the bells for early service. Alexander Burnham was standing in the chancel ready to make the ways of righteousness appear amiable to his flock and to speak, out of his knowledge, of the peace that passed understanding.

She felt alert and collected.

But in an odd and bitter way she felt disappointed too. Why had she returned to this small, restricted, accustomed place? She had been free. She had breathed upland air. Why had she not gone on and scaled the glassy mountains and seen what lay beyond?

Sunlight flooded the window. The red paper school-house in the dish-garden was incandescent. Why, there it is, she thought. There is Life.

She thought of all the children she had pruned and polished and kept in line, and to whom she had explained, by precept and example, the hard, the true, the simple and beautiful meaning of the human adventure. She thought of their faces lighting up with fresh wonder when they conceived, for the first time, the roundness of the earth. Of those who had gone and of those—if she dared hope—who were yet to come. For a scandalized instant, before she forgot it entirely and forever, she recalled the amorality she had been on the verge of uttering to those desk-jumping children in her dream.

She knew, with a passion of yearning, exactly where she wished to go. Not to old Cathay. Not to London or Paris or to the anomalous country beyond the hills. She wanted to walk down Oakwood, across LaFayette, up Maple, over to Grant (nodding to William Holloway) and into the portals of Cedar Grove School. She wanted to go into the geography room. To put her hat and gloves and bag in the cupboard. To unroll the big map of the world. To mount her platform and to stand there waiting for the first graders to file in—abandoning folly as they crossed her sill, greeting her soberly, one by one, in the prescribed words which told her that the day had begun to blossom.

Billie Jean was tidying the bureau. On her left hand a single diamond sparkled. She pushed the potted azalea back so far that it tilted the mirror and Miss Dove could see the nurse's reflection and that of Thomas Baker as he came into the room.

Thomas' face looked tired, like the face of a man who has forgotten about sleep. But it looked jaunty, as well—the way it had looked, she remembered, when a hard test or a baseball game had come out better than he'd had a right to expect. In the crook of either arm he carried a bundle wrapped in a blue blanket.

(Twins, thought Miss Dove. Boy twins. I shall have to keep them apart—one on the first row and one far over by the windows—even though that upsets my alphabetical seating arrangement. But would they—? Would she ever—? Hadn't something been said— something in Thomas' voice—about strangeness and benignity?)

Beneath the sheet she moved her hand slowly, fearfully, toward her right thigh. She held her thumb and forefinger curved, like a crab's pincers, in pinching position. One tweak and she would know! But suddenly she let her fingers go limp and her hand lie still. Investigation was not a patient's province.

Thomas had paused just inside the door. When he saw in the glass Billie Jean's delighted smile, he wagged his ears. He cocked one eyebrow. "What a man among men am I!" his clowning plainly bragged.

He tiptoed to the bedside. The babies began to cry.

217

"An-ha-n-n! Ahan-a-n-nn-n!" their shrill, indignant voices went.

"Quiet, please," said Miss Dove.

Nobody—not she nor Thomas nor Billie Jean—was surprised when the babies hushed.

She gazed up at the doctor. Her eyes were gray and luminous and steady. She waited to hear the truth.

Thomas returned her gaze. His face, like the paper schoolhouse, seemed to glow from within.

He thought of what Adams Temple had said about Aeneas and Anchises and the rounded circle. He thought of Miss Dove tying Jincey's hair with the string. He saw her, standing straight as her long map-pointer, beside the desk and the globe. Then he told her what she wanted to know. He told her without wasting a word.

He stood erect. He drew a curtain of gravity over his face, making it blank of everything except decorum and sober dedication. In the reserved, deferential, un-inflected accents of Cedar Grove Elementary School, he spoke at last.

"Good morning, Miss Dove," he said.